∨P

P9-BIV-150

STAMPEDE!

Moses Quinta turned and watched young Sara Farnsworth and her dappled pinto work through scattered bunches of cattle grazing in the clearing. Suddenly the sharp crackle of gunfire came from the north edge and the next instant cattle were exploding through the trees. Behind the cattle appeared four horsemen holding revolvers that spouted flame and the terrified animals broke to the south, flinging powdery snow skyward in a lumbering run that brought them down toward the campsite.

Immediately, Quinta knew his men couldn't make it to their horses in time. They turned and ran through the deep snow toward the boulders by the creek. And when Quinta looked back at the clearing, it was to see Sara Farnsworth's pinto bucking and fighting the bit before it was swept away in a solid mass of stampeding cattle. . . .

TALES OF THE OLD WEST

SPIRIT WARRIOR (1795, $2.50)
by G. Clifton Wisler
The only settler to survive the savage indian attack was a little boy. Although raised as a red man, every man was his enemy when the two worlds clashed — but he vowed no man would be his equal.

IRON HEART (1736, $2.25)
by Walt Denver
Orphaned by an indian raid, Ben vowed he'd never rest until he'd brought death to the Arapahoes. And it wasn't long before they came to fear the rider of vengeance they called . . . Iron Heart.

WEST OF THE CIMARRON (1681, $2.50)
by G. Clifton Wisler
Eric didn't have a chance revenging his father's death against the Dunstan gang until a stranger with a fast draw and a dark past arrived from West of the Cimarron.

BIG HORN GUNFIGHTER (1975, $2.50)
by Robert Kamman
Quinta worked for both sides of the law, and he left a trail of graves from old Mexico to Wyoming to prove it. His partner cut and run, so Quinta took the law into his own hands. Because the only law that mattered to a gunfighter was measured in calibers.

BLOOD TRAIL SOUTH (1349, $2.25)
by Walt Denver
John Rustin was left for dead, his wife and son butchered by six hard-cases. Five years later, someone with cold eyes and hot lead pursued those six murdering coyotes. Was it a lawman — or John Rustin, himself?

Available wherever paperbacks are sold, or order direct from the Publisher. Send cover price plus 50¢ per copy for mailing and handling to Zebra Books, Dept. 1975, 475 Park Avenue South, New York, N.Y. 10016. Residents of New York, New Jersey and Pennsylvania must include sales tax. DO NOT SEND CASH.

BIG HORN GUNFIGHTER

ROBERT KAMMEN

ZEBRA BOOKS
KENSINGTON PUBLISHING CORP.

ZEBRA BOOKS

are published by

Kensington Publishing Corp.
475 Park Avenue South
New York, NY 10016

Copyright © 1987 by Robert Kammen

All rights reserved. No part of this book may be reproduced
in any form or by any means without the prior written
consent of the Publisher, excepting brief quotes used in
reviews.

First printing: January 1987

Printed in the United States of America

1

When word was carried into Laramie by a trustee named Blackie that the renowned gunfighter Moses Quinta was coming out, a crowd began gathering in front of Dumont's General Store, the first business place giving those who waited a glimpse of the gravel road winding down from the territorial prison. Usually the release of a prisoner was an unheralded event, with the freed man slinking along back streets to the train depot where he'd catch the first piece of rolling stock away from a place he'd learned to hate.

Inside the sanctuary of his store, Ira Dumont leaned on a counter while scanning the contents of an article about the gunfighter in an old edition of the *Cheyenne Star*, the gist of it stating that Moses Quinta had been apprehended in Cheyenne and sent to territorial prison without benefit of a trial. It was in the saloons that the storekeeper had come across this last piece of information, learned further that when the gunfighter appeared, men were either killed or sent to prison, because Quinta worked on both sides of the law. That must be gospel, pondered Dumont, since it was the governor who'd signed the writ of habeas corpus giving Quinta his

5

freedom. Further down on the front page was a picture showing Quinta handcuffed between two U.S. marshals.

There he was, three months ago:

Moses Quinta, manacled hands hooked into his gun belt, standing some four inches taller than the other men; the black sombrero shading slate-gray eyes; the tanned flesh lying taut against the bony contours of the angular face and shaggy mustache concealing his upper lip; dark coat over a light cotton shirt and a silky kerchief at his neck; the leather holsters empty but thonged down at their lower ends; the gray trousers coming down over roweled boots hand-crafted by a Texas bootmaker. A smile seemed to sparkle out of the gunfighter's eyes, as if he knew that wrong had been done to him.

"A killer," was the storekeeper's terse comment, as he folded the newspaper and set it aside. Ira Dumont was no bigger than a circus dwarf, with gnomelike features on a head too large for his body and a deformed foot encased in a special-made shoe. He'd used a quick wit and sharp business acumen to turn what had once been a deserted building partially razed by fire into a moneymaking venture. Being somewhat of a historian, Dumont knew that down through the ages kings and warlords used to confide in dwarfs because of the mystical qualities supposedly attached to these people, and after twelve years here he knew most of Laramie's secrets. When asked why he left Utah, Ira Dumont would solemnly reply that he'd been blacklisted by the Mormon sect. That had been in his wild, womanizing days, he liked to say, before striking eastward as dictated by the flip of a silver dollar. Somehow he'd wound up here.

"Someone's coming!"

Dumont strolled to a front window as the eyes of those

6

gathered along the boardwalks swung to the road leading up to the greystone walls of the prison, a good quarter of a mile to the southeast.

Before, there'd been idle talk and some jokes being bantered about, with the crowd more concerned about the heat or the price of beef—now only the gusty wind could be heard shrilling under the covered boardwalks or causing loose roof shingles or window shutters to bang against the buildings. A tumbleweed bounced onto Main Street to tumble against the legs of a rancher who jumped aside as though it were snake-laden, the man's eyes never leaving the road. The faces of others showed awe or fear or uncertainty, along with anger and just plain hatred. To the storekeeper's way of thinking it was as if the angel of light was a-coming to claim his own, that before this day ended there'd be killing.

"It's him—whose picture I seen in the paper. Quinta!"

"But he ain't armed?"

"Probably carrying his guns in that satchel!"

Mostly there were townspeople, a sprinkling of ranchers and assorted riffraff, and with four hardcases clustered across the street in front of the Elkhart Saloon. The sight of Moses Quinta striding purposely along that dusty road held the crowd immobile, the fear of the man rippling upstreet like the stench of carrion being carried into town by the quartering wind. Little rivulets of dust popped out from under the gunfighter's boots, and when Quinta's long stride carried him into shadow cast by Dumont's store, some of the more timid souls slunk back into buildings. And if humiliation was the name of the game, or the hatred of those wanting him dead, it didn't seem to be making any inroads as to what was going on behind Moses Quinta's passive expression, for he could be going to church, or courting, for all the attention he paid to those watching him. Opposite, one of the hardcases stepped to the edge of the boardwalk and let his hand hover near his holstered Navy Colt, but the spell cast by Quinta, that of a man taking a casual stroll through a ghost town, unnerved the hardcase, and he eased back into shadow. Then Moses Quinta was at the first intersection and veering onto a side street that would take him to the train depot, and leaving in his wake men still gripped with the hatred and fear of him, and grudging admiration, too.

Mainly because of its location, the Laramie Hotel, an elegant, two-storied structure facing the railroad center, rarely had an empty room, but when Moses Quinta came strolling into its lobby the clerk on duty paled some before muttering timorously, "You can have the President Grant suite, Mr. Quinta."

"A room'll do." He reached for the quilled pen.

"All—all of the rooms are occupied."

Casting the clerk a hard scowl, he said, "The suite, then." He scrawled a fancy Q and dropped the pen on the register book. "I'm wanting to take a hot bath right away. After that, I expect to see a couple of bottles of Red Dog whiskey and a steak with all the trimmings waiting in my suite. And I'm a-wanting to see Ira Dumont."

"Dumont?"

"The storekeeper, boy. Send someone reliable over to fetch him. Just make damned certain you or whoever you send"—fishing out a silver dollar, he slapped it down on the counter top—"keeps quiet about this. I've been a little edgy of late."

The clerk eased backwards as Quinta reached around and lifted out a box of imported Havana cigars. "Put

8

them on my bill. Now, where's that suite?"

"It's upstairs," exclaimed the clerk as he started out from behind the counter.

"I'll find it," Quinta said flatly, and headed for the staircase.

Dust filmed what furniture there was in the suite, and Moses Quinta knew that it hadn't been occupied for some time. As was his habit, he checked out all the rooms, locking those doors opening onto the hallway and keeping from being framed in the windows when he secured the latches. He hadn't reached the aging side of his thirties by being careless, and from the reception he'd just received from the citizens of Laramie, could be that someone might try to take him out here at the hotel. Others had tried, in the past, and Moses Quinta had left a trail of graves from down Old Mexico way to places further north of his present location. It wasn't something to brag on, nor did he ever kill a man who wasn't asking for killing. He always hired out to the high bidder. Holding up banks or stagecoaches, he'd found out early on, wasn't too profitable, but doing the work of money men was, and a helluva lot safer.

There he'd been, loafing about Dodge City, easing out of bed around noon, and after a nice hot bath and shave, he'd generally head over to the gambling houses. Then a letter had caught up with him, and even before he opened it Moses Quinta had a premonition of impending doom. First of all, the envelope had borne a Wyoming postmark, which should have been reason enough to discard it; the contents of the letter told of how a widow woman up in Big Horn basin country was fighting to hold onto her ranch, and of how she would pay a tolerable sum to Quinta if he'd hire out to her. That letter had been

9

headed for the trash barrel until a final paragraph caught the gunfighter's eye, in which the widow woman told how a cattle baron with the fancy handle of Charlton Talbot was trying to force her out.

"Charlton Talbot," he said bitterly. Talbot was the reason he'd spent five years in a Texas prison. They'd only gotten around seven thousand in that bank robbery, but more than enough to turn Talbot into a rancher. At the time they'd been a couple of wild yonkers out of Oklahoma. There was good old Charlton with those big, luminous blue eyes that women adored and kind of pale-complexioned so that they wanted to take him home to cuddle, with those bank tellers always figuring Charlton to be collecting for the Salvation Army until he pulled out that old Dragoon and demanded their money. There'd been two bank robberies, one successful, the other seeing Moses Quinta shot and abandoned by his partner.

In the southwest bedroom, Quinta dropped the satchel on the metal-framed bed and peeled out of the suit coat and thin flannel shirt presented to him by the territory of Wyoming upon his being released from prison. He gazed at the mirror reflecting the puckered scar at his right side, the wound given him by his old partner, Charlton Talbot. He was much leaner, harder, than he'd been three months ago; sledgehammering rocks would do that to a man. Those prison guards were a vicious lot, the hot, dry summers and long winters having sucked any human decency out of them, and hankering to use those bullwhips to goad a man into working harder. One of them, a squat hunk of nothing, bragged that he'd been using weights to build up his muscles. The man's arrogant manner got to Moses Quinta, who found out in a bare-knuckle match that the guard couldn't fight his way out of a bagful of goat shit. It had been a short walk from there to solitary for Quinta, with only the release notice brought by his lawyer saving him from getting worked over by the other guards.

"Hell," he remarked sagely, "Sunday school teachers just couldn't cut the mustard in that hellhole." And someone with a lot of political clout had arranged for him to be arrested, the threads of Quinta's suspicions pointing to his old sidekick, Talbot. That three-month exposure to territorial hospitality was another reason for helping the widow woman, and it had left Quinta a lot meaner.

Opening the satchel, he pulled out the pair of holstered .45 Colt Peacemakers with their black gutta-percha grips and a two-shot derringer, before proceeding to dump the rest of the satchel's contents on the bed. There was a rap at the door in the living room, a woman announcing that his bath was ready in a room just across the corridor.

"Obliged," he yelled back, while turning to the business of checking out the loads in the Colts. Three months was a long time not to handle them, and they felt awkward to hold. Shucking out of his boots, he lit a cigar and thrust the Colts into his waistband as he left the bedroom and opened the door opening onto the corridor where he found the clerk who'd rented him the suite standing there holding two bottles of Red Dog whiskey. He took one of the bottles, told the clerk to leave the other in the suite.

The bathroom was about twelve feet square with walls painted a yellowy white and oblong windows letting in midday sunlight, the window to the east having its bottom half pushed up and a balcony running under it.

11

Vaporous steam rose from scalding hot water filling the wooden-stave washtub and burning wood crackled in the potbellied stove, the combination of the heat and the small room causing sweat to pop out on Quinta's face as he pulled a chair close to the washtub and set his Colts on it so that their grips faced the tub. Undressing, he settled gingerly into the tub, the open door leading into the hallway and both windows within eyesight.

Almost immediately the soothing water began to chase tension from muscles hardened by pounding rocks and to cleanse skin that hadn't seen the insides of a place like this for three months. He began to feel drowsy, but with his senses alert to sounds within the hotel, the rumble of a passing train, other outside noises.

Though Quinta heard two men chatting as they moved up the staircase just down the hall, the window to the east held his gaze. Again came the chink-chink of spurs, and the gunfighter knew that someone was out on the balcony.

"Damned shame a man can't even take a bath," he muttered, reaching with his right hand for one of the Colts, his attention momentarily distracted by the sight of a limping man somewhat short of stature hammering on the door of Quinta's suite.

"You the storekeeper?"

"Ah, there you are, Mr. Quinta." A nervous Ira Dumont swept the hat from his head and gestured with it at the other man who'd just moved into view. "This is—"

"Haskins of the *Denver Gazette*," the other man said pompously. "You're news, Mr. Quinta—yessiree, front page stuff."

Later on the storekeeper, Dumont, would say that what transpired next happened so quickly that it defied describing, though he would say later, too, that he'd stood there rock-steady when Moses Quinta shot at and killed a man who suddenly stood framed in the window to the east, the ambusher's weapon barking to scour a groove in the varnished hallway floor next to Dumont. The truth of what happened was that as Quinta spun in the washtub to place a slug in the stranger's throat, reporter Haskins from the *Denver Gazette* was flopping downward to shatter the lens in his horn-rimmed glasses, the storekeeper sprawling alongside, but still catching a glimpse of Moses Quinta lunging naked out of the tub and darting over to lean out the open window. There was a split second when Quinta hesitated as another ambusher tried to slip back through another window in his efforts to get away. But the meanness Quinta had been storing up in prison caused his trigger finger to move before he could react to its pressure, with a slug from his Colt slapping into the man's back to leave him wedged dead over the window sill.

"Picked a bad time to rile me up, stranger," he said angrily as he swung his upper body back into the washroom. He eased back into the tub as Dumont and the reporter groped upright. "Get in here, Dumont, and lock that damned door."

The storekeeper hurried into the room and closed the door. He said shakily, "Mr. Quinta, I'll swear it was self-defense."

"That's mighty noble of you, storekeeper; just tell that to the marshal." Quinta laid his gun down on the chair. "By your sign you sell guns."

"Yes, the finest money can buy."

"We'll talk about that later. Right now I want you to trot back to your store and fetch me some new clothes.

Lost a little weight in the last few months, so make them about a half-size smaller than what I've been wearing."

"Just what manner of clothes did you have in mind?"

"Traveling clothes, storekeeper. The best you've got. Upon your return we'll discuss some other items I'll be needing." Reaching to the chair for his trousers draped over its back, he handed them to Dumont and settled deeper into the tub. "You'll find the other half of that monkey suit in my suite."

A skeptical town marshal had finally taken the word of the storekeeper and Haskins, the reporter from the *Denver Gazette*, just to why there were two dead men waiting to be carted off the the F.L. Prickett Funeral Home, one body still draped over the windowsill, the other ambusher having fallen off the balcony to land on the front steps of the Laramie Hotel, much to the discomfort of an immigrant family from Germany who'd been entering the hotel at the time.

At the moment Moses Quinta was standing before the dresser mirror in his bedroom, checking over his appearance. Although the new woolen shirt fitted him, it reeked of mothballs, while the Levi's were a little stiff, but it felt good to get rid of the other clothes. There was also a bandana, which he tied around his neck and adjusted, and a cattleman's leather coat supple to the touch with his derringer nestling in an inner pocket. He'd worn out his hand-tooled narrow-toed boots in prison, and the ones Dumont had brought along were a little snug, but usage would break them in, Quinta figured, as he picked up his gun belt and buckled it around his waist.

It was about an hour on the dark side of sundown, and

14

Quinta had lighted what coal oil lamps there were in the suite, left some of the shades up for the benefit of those who might still be interested in his present whereabouts. Those ambushers must have been sent by the same person or persons who were responsible for his stay at the territorial prison, but if Charlton Talbot was behind this, it meant that others knew about the letter mailed to him by the widow woman.

"So much for the sanctity of the mails," Quinta said as he eased the tan Stetson over his head. A rapping sound brought him to the next room to a door, which he opened to find a woman of indeterminate age smiling at him. As she flounced past him into the suite, Quinta had the notion that she looked a little garish in that red-corseted dress, matching bonnet and dyed red hair.

"A pleasure meeting you, Mr. Quinta." Her voice had a hard, gravelly tint to it.

"The pleasure's all mine."

"I will be spending the night?" The smile she had for Quinta came from lips coated with too much lipstick. "I'm Hattie Mayfield."

"You will, Hattie, unless your ma told you to be home before curfew."

With a laugh for him she stepped over to the liquor cabinet and filled a glass nearly to its brim with Red Dog whiskey. "It'll cost you more, my man." And uttering that, Hattie Mayfield, who'd just moved to Laramie after a brief stint at the copper town of Butte and was now gainfully employed by a local house of pleasure, brought the glass to her lips.

"Figured that," Quinta said pleasantly.

"So"—she swept the bonnet from her head and let it flutter onto the davenport—"just take your hat off, Mr.

15

Quinta, and we'll make ourselves comfortable."

"Tell you what, Hattie, just make yourself to home until I get back." He escorted the woman into the bedroom he'd been using. "It'll probably take an hour or two to transact some important business."

"Really, I am disappointed."

"Well, now, don't fret none about that. But there are those who're trying to keep track of my whereabouts—so maybe you could help me out."

"Anything, Mr. Quinta."

"These people would sure enough think I'm still here if you'd sorta undress in front of that window over there."

"It'll cost you more for games like that."

"Sure, no problem," Quinta said easily. "Then, after I'm gone, how's about crawling into that bed and sort of pretend like I'm making love to you. You know, Hattie, you could sort of moan and stir that bed about some."

"Oh, Mr. Quinta, I just know this is going to be a profitable evening."

"For both of us, I'm a-hoping. But money's no object when a pretty filly like you'll be waiting when I get back. Now, there's plenty of whiskey. Be back quick as I can."

Quinta eased into the hallway, going along it to a back door which brought him onto an outer staircase, and he clambered down. The alley he followed ran to the north where a few houses were located, along with a storage shed owned by the storekeeper, Dumont. Crickets were chirping down by a creek hidden by shadows and two horses tied to a tree shied away when Quinta's soft whistle brought the storekeeper out of the shed.

"You're late," complained Dumont.

"Some," admitted Quinta as he checked the cinch on

16

the saddled horse, the other horse having the supplies he'd ordered from the storekeeper packed on its back. He turned to Dumont and lit a cigar. "Found out some interesting things about you whilst I was in prison. Mostly that you've been padding the accounts of your customers. Those folks who run the territorial prison won't like that if word was to get out."

"Sir, that's a damned lie!"

"I figure it's stealing, Dumont. There's a possibility you could be pounding rocks too. But you might consider what I'm about to do stealing." Quinta untied the reins of both horses and swung into the saddle of the gray.

"Hold on now," blustered Dumont. "I demand my money!"

"Storekeeper, those who arrested me down at Cheyenne confiscated my worldly possessions—damned unkindly of them. So's I figure if you was to head over to Cheyenne and claim my property, we'll be even."

"You damned crook!" shouted Ira Dumont, pulling out a Hammond Bulldog pistol. "I demand to be paid!"

The gunfighter dragged deeply on the cigar, the glowing end of it revealing his bone-white teeth and the contempt he felt for the storekeeper in his eyes. "Put that toy away, Dumont, or there'll be another body stretched out at the funeral parlor—yours, I reckon."

"You—you—damnable crook."

"Some folks would say that," muttered Quinta as he swung the gray away from the tree and began riding away.

Ira Dumont fired at the gunfighter's indistinct form, only to have the slug strike the high branch of a tree. When he cocked the gun to fire again, Quinta had vanished.

And in leaving Laramie, the gunfighter Moses Quinta

added three more people to the long list of those who hated him. Ira Dumont, stung by Quinta's thievery, did take the stage to Cheyenne the following morning to claim the gunfighter's property. The hotel clerk who'd rented the President Grant suite to Quinta had his pay docked before he was fired. And by the time Moses Quinta reached the Laramie River some three hours later and bedded down for the night, he was wondering if Hattie Mayfield was still moaning and rolling about in that bed.

"Serves them right for not checking out my references." And uttering that, Moses Quinta took another long swig of Red Dog whiskey before falling into an untroubled sleep.

2

From a distance the horseman sitting slouched in the saddle while surveying a timber-littered track rising between two peaks in the Big Horn range could be just another cowhand letting his bronc take a breather. But the leather-gloved hands rolling a cigarette into shape were small and supple, while closer now, a person would notice the chestnut hair piled up under the work-worn hat, the high cheekbones and hazel eyes squinting into concentration in an attempt to catch sight of any cattle that might be lurking in the thick underbrush.

A large bandana was tied snugly around Celia Farnsworth's neck, the outer end of it brushing against the leather jacket under which she had on a plaid shirt; over her Levi's she had on leather chaps with scuffed boots thrust into the stirrups of her Texas saddle. Necessity had made Celia Farnsworth a marksman, with either the Winchester resting in the saddle boot or the holstered Smith & Wesson.

Up here in Big Horn Basin country those who knew Celia Farnsworth considered her a strong-willed woman, and maybe too stubborn for her own good, and that of her three daughters growing rapidly into womanhood themselves. Ever since her husband, Buck, had been killed three years ago, she'd been ramrodding the 77 Ranch, a sizable chore for a man, harder for a woman. But Celia wasn't the complaining kind, even though her problems were of a twofold nature—a lack of ready cash and manpower. Those willing to work for her had been scared off by cattle baron Charlton Talbot, and without these men, Celia knew that she wouldn't be able to drive her cattle to the railhead at Sheridan before summer ran its long, hot course.

"Kiyeee!" Beth Farnsworth, Celia's oldest daughter and a month shy of her eighteenth birthday, emerged from the brush on her paint to spin her lariat in wide circles about her head before casting it over the horns of a large steer. A hard tug at the reins brought the paint back on its haunches, with the rope going taut as the steer hit the end of it and spun sideways before dropping onto its side. Before it could scramble up from the ground, Celia Farnsworth flicked the lariat she'd been holding down to heel the animal, the rope tightening around the steer's hind legs.

Several yards away and on a lower elevation of the draw, Amanda Farnsworth pulled one of the branding irons out of the fire she was tending. She ran over to the steer and there was the smell of burning hide when she pressed the hot iron against the right flank of the steer, holding it there for a couple of seconds before lifting it away.

As Celia Farnsworth watched her daughter, Amanda, hurry back to the fire, it was with the sobering realization that they were doing dangerous work. Although they were looking for cattle on land she owned, the source of Celia's worry was the law passed a couple of years ago by the territorial legislation, whereby only members of the Wyoming Stock Growers Association could round up unbranded cattle. These so-called mavericks were then divided among members of the association, which up here in the basin meant Charlton Talbot and his T-Bar Ranch. And at any time one of those stock detectives Talbot had hired could happen by.

"Well," she said firmly and silently, "I'll brand anything growing hair that happens onto my land."

Her dislike for Talbot, a relative newcomer to the basin, had hardened into hatred ever since her husband's body was found up at Nowood Creek, along with a running iron bearing an obscure brand and used by those who'd killed Buck Farnsworth. It was Celia's contention that the iron had been deliberately left behind by Talbot's men. When a deputy U.S. marshal arrived about two weeks later it was to find that a summer rainstorm had erased any tracks.

Celia coiled her lariat as she helped Beth Farnsworth herd the steer down the draw to where her youngest daughter, Sara, was keeping watch over the other cattle they'd found. As the steer merged with the others, Celia reined up and draped her hands over the pommel, her eyes going to shadows beginning to crawl up the lower reaches of the Big Horns. Eighteen years ago she'd gotten her first glimpse of these mountains that would become such a large part of her life. Every dawning her eyes sought them, and with each season change the coloration of these lofty peaks underwent change also, as if the mood of the Big Horns held sway over the weather. There were yarns of those who'd gone up there, either hunting or after stray cattle, and were never seen again. Only to herself would Celia Farnsworth admit that she feared these jagged heights, for oftentimes she felt them calling out to her, as if somehow her destiny and that of the 77 spread was intermingled with these mountains. A shiver of unease ran through Celia's mind as she spurred her grulla up the draw toward the fire.

"Amanda," she called out, "let's call it a day." Dismounting by the fire, she helped her daughter kick sand over its flames, with the branding irons lying nearby cooling off.

Celia Farnsworth held a tight rein over her daughters, though she would loosen it from time to time because she realized they hadn't gotten over the sudden death of their father. She studied Amanda, an impish, impulsive and golden-haired young woman of seventeen. For the last few weeks Amanda's sunny smile had been missing because the young man who'd been sparking her would be leaving the basin once his father sold their homestead some twenty miles north of here. Talbot was literally forcing these people out, Celia knew, and the thought rankled her. She'd liked what she'd seen of young Tim Petrie, and it was Celia's notion that he'd make a fine husband for Amanda. But Tim was leaving, and in time her daughter would find another young man.

They gathered up the branding irons and rode down to where the others were waiting with the cattle, and there, Celia turned affectionate eyes upon Sara, a gangling girl of sixteen with her mother's chestnut hair, Buck's dark brown eyes. Like the others, Sara had on the working gear of a cowhand. Up to now Sara didn't seem to be too interested in the opposite sex, though Celia felt the signs were there. But ask Sara Farnsworth to go hunting or fishing and all talk of boys would end.

After they'd brought the cattle at a walk along the

falling reaches of the draw, Celia reined over to ride beside Beth, of the light brown hair hanging in braids over her shoulders, sunburnt oval face and band of freckles showing plain. She was almost as shapely as her mother, though smaller through the bust.

"I've been meaning to talk."

"About Raoul I suppose?"

"Girl, I just don't like him working for Talbot."

"Jobs are hard to come by."

"We need help."

"We can't afford to pay what the T-Bar does."

"Do you love him?" Celia asked bluntly.

"I—Ma, I think I do."

"He could be spying for the T-Bar."

"Not Raoul!"

"Charlton Talbot," Celia said chillily, "is doing all he can to drive us out of the basin. When was the last time you saw Raoul Dixon?"

"Last month—in Silver Springs."

"I'm not blind, child," murmured Celia. "I know you've been meeting him over by the river. But just remember, Beth, we're fighting for survival. I'm not saying that you can't see Raoul again. I just don't want you telling him about our plans to drive the herd to Sheridan."

"I understand, Ma, it's just . . ."

Celia patted her daughter on the arm. "I know— you're coming onto womanhood. You wish things were . . . better." Then Celia swung her horse after some cattle beginning to drift toward the underbrush, while Amanda and Sara fanned out on the other side, and with the foothills opening up to them. On these higher elevations a cooler wind rustled around them than they'd find out on the plains. A few clouds were showing, with no definite pattern to them, and the sun was standing just over the Absarokas, the mountain range guarding the western reaches of the basin, a good sixty miles away. The Big Horn River cut through the heart of the basin, feeding others such as the Owl Creek, Greybull, Shoshone, and in turn, meltoff flowing down from the mountains was the true sustainer of life out here. Guarding the basin to the south were the Owl Creek and Bridger mountains, with Charlton Talbot's T-Bar spread located there, its boundaries sweeping northward in the cattle baron's attempts to extend what he owned by buying or forcing others out.

Framing a mental picture of the cattle baron, she saw: Charlton Talbot easing off his thoroughbred stallion in front of the Ranchester Saloon in Silver Springs, the gold-headed cane with a few diamonds sparkling in it held in one hand as one of his hired guns took the reins from him; cynical blue eyes under the pearl-gray cattleman's hat sweeping coldly over a town he controlled; a tailored western suit covering the thickening frame, and the dust seeming to slip away from the fancy boots. The rancher had never married, but kept a woman in Silver Springs and one over to Greybull. More than once she'd thought about parting Charlton Talbot's thick black hair with a slug from her Smith & Wesson, but those hired guns were always around.

Before his death, Buck Farnsworth had tried to talk the other ranchers into standing up to the T-Bar. And he'd been their spokesman at cattleman's meetings held in Silver Springs. Sometimes, Celia recalled, he'd come home from one of those meetings and stomp angrily around the ranch house, damning the other ranchers for their lack of intestinal fortitude, as he called it. But after simmering down, Buck Farnsworth would quietly say to his wife that their neighbors were peaceful men suddenly confronted with evil. And before Talbot settled in the basin there'd been marauding bands of Indians, winters so fiercely cold and stormy that cattle would freeze standing still, and with ranches so far from civilization that it took the better part of a week to ride over and back from Buffalo for supplies. But it was the way her husband, the others, wanted it, rubbing shoulders with the mountain ranges, breathing air untarnished by laws or politicians, just plain being free men. There'd been a price to pay, and Celia Farnsworth would gladly pay it again just to have her husband and a few years back. But now was now, and she'd fight that sonofabitch Talbot to her dying gasp.

They brought the bunch of cattle splashing across Nowood Creek and further out on the prairie where those they'd found today went lowing toward the main herd had scattered some and were grazing as the shadows of twilight drifted around them. With Beth Farnsworth spurring ahead, the others rode westward along the creek until they reached a gentle hillock giving them a glimpse of the 77 ranchsite sheltered by mesas to the northwest. Horses milled about in one of the pole corrals. There was no sign of movement around the bunkhouse squatting under a huge oak tree nor further along at the blacksmith shop, a square, open-sided building. But sparrows were darting out of the open hayloft door of the hip-roofed barn, the wall paint peeling and the lustre gone from it. The fieldstone ranch house had a look of permanence to it, as if it had always been there, but the pair of horses switching their tails at the hitching post in front of the house hadn't, nor had the man stretched out in the hammock on the front porch with his hat pulled over his face.

Reaching down for her Winchester, Celia leveled a shell into its breech and said calmly, "Keep me covered, girls."

Touching spurs to her grulla, Celia rode down the slope and onto the lane curling toward the pole fence hemming in the buildings. After passing through the gate, a chicken went squawking out her way as Celia swung to the ground to let the reins drop while heading toward the house with the rifle coming to bear on the stranger. Right off anger simmered in Celia's eyes when she spotted the empty whiskey bottle resting on the man's chest, and with his drunken snoring coming to her loud and kind of raspy, like the stranger's mouth was full of phlegm. The brands on the horses were unknown to her, but those long sack-encased items on the packhorse had the familiar shapes of rifles.

"Some drunken gun dealer," was Celia Farnsworth's scorning assessment. Swiveling the barrel of her Winchester upward, she fired over the house, the crackling sound of it making the horses shy away, but the stranger just settled deeper into the hammock while a drunken burp came out from under the covering of his dusty hat.

Spinning around on her two-inch heels, Celia waved in her daughters while striding angrily over to the well, with a windmill rising over it, the gusting wind turning the upper wheel and fluttering the tail vane. She pumped water into a pail, then trudged back and up the steps of the porch and dumped the pail of chilling water over the sleeping man.

Moses Quinta's flailing arms knocked the hat away, the sudden movement of his arms and body turning the hammock over and spilling him onto the porch. Gasping, he stared up through red-rimmed eyes at the blurred image of Celia Farnsworth standing over him.

"I don't like drunks, mister! So get on your horse and skedaddle!"

"What they say about you . . . in Silver Springs," rasped Quinta as he shook the water out of his hair and spat some out of his mouth, "is true."

"That being?"

"That you're a hard-headed, cantankerous . . . woman!" Grabbing his hat, he pulled himself erect and jammed it over his head to match his glare with hers.

"Is that so?" Celia levered the Winchester again.

"Damnit, I wouldn't be a-standing here wet and trail-weary if'n I hadn't 've gotten your letter, Mrs. Farnsworth."

"I'll be damned. You're—"

"Moses Quinta." He pulled a wet cigar out of his shirt pocket and threw it a sorrowful glance before tossing it down.

Pursing her lips in disgust, Celia Farnsworth said icily, "From all those stories told about you, I expected more."

3

Moses Quinta was still simmering over the caustic remarks made by the ranchwoman that he'd have to shave and take a bath down at the creek before she'd let him sit at her table. And in the bunkhouse Quinta was muttering to himself that he wasn't about to share his bath with frogs or tadpoles, or any water snake that might slither by. The coal oil lamp hanging suspended from a wall peg cast light upon the mirror Quinta was standing before as he brought the straight razor toward his lathered face. Through a nearby window came diminishing shards of daylight, alpenglow outlining jagged peaks. The bunkhouse had the feel of a place that hadn't been occupied for a spell, but Quinta could tell that it had been tended to, and there were hunks of wood in the bin by the potbellied stove.

An errant stroke caused Quinta to grimace and he used a finger to brush away the beads of blood coming from the small nick on his cheek, the slight pain turning his thoughts to the woman again, and her dousing him with that pail of water.

"Damned outstandish for a woman needing help. By rights I should saddle up and head for safer parts." But

Quinta knew that when he headed north out of Laramie he'd bought chips in the game between the Farnsworth woman and Charlton Talbot. Somehow it was divine intervention her mentioning Talbot in that letter she'd sent him. Maybe a dozen years ago he would have headed straight for Talbot's ranch and had it out with the man. But with age had come caution, his desire to avenge what Talbot had done to him tempered by the fact that he could make a tidy sum out of this by striking a deal with the ranchwoman, maybe enough to open his own gambling house—that Jackson Hole country was wide open, he'd heard.

Quinta surveyed his smoothly shaven face before he used the straight razor to trim his mustache, those strands of dark brown hair growing shaggy over his ears and along the sideburns. Wiping himself dry, he donned his shirt, the gleam in his eyes for the bottle of Red Dog lying next to his holstered guns on the iron cot.

"With a disposition such as that woman's got," remarked Quinta, leaning to pick up the bottle and uncork it, "she'll probably serve old harness leather for supper." Though the gunfighter couldn't recall the last time he'd had a home-cooked meal, the thought of what was to come caused him to lower the amber contents of the bottle a good two inches. Grimacing, he corked the bottle and tossed it down and reached for his hat while ambling outside.

On the front porch, the hammock reminded him of Celia Farnsworth's hostile nature, and he hesitated before rapping on the oaken door panes. When the door finally opened, he fumbled off his hat and said to Celia, "Ah—sure appreciate this invite to chow down."

"Out here we call it supper," Celia said tartly as she

30

motioned him inside.

Moses Quinta was surprised to see the lacy curtains over the windows and throw rugs on the varnished hardwood floor, the flowers in two vases on opposite ends of the mantelpiece over the glowing fireplace. Dropping his hat on a chair, he looked at Celia still wearing her work clothes. Though she'd combed her hair, she wore no makeup, and now Quinta mentioned the fact that the large, round oaken table only had two place settings.

"Quinta, men like you have roving eyes," Celia said acidly as they settled down across from one another at the table, and though Quinta remained silent, there was a flare of resentment.

He said, "Meaning your daughters?"

"And you have an unsavory reputation."

"Well, now," he said crossly, "done some things I ain't proud of. But the fortunes of life can change a man—make him ornery . . . or downright uncaring." Hungrily his eyes went to the bowls of mashed potatoes, brown gravy, carrots swimming in cream sauce, and the steaks still simmering and heaped on a meat platter.

"You've killed too, I've heard."

Reluctantly his eyes swung away from the food. "Why, only in self-defense, ma'am." Now the gentle breeze coming in the open windows brought the aroma of the steaks his way. "Food just might get cold with all this . . . palavering."

"Self-defense?" spoke Celia again. "Men like you never kill that way. To tell you the truth, Quinta, I just don't like you."

Running an irritated finger along his mustache, and with his temper flaring, Quinta replied, "Can't exactly say I cotton to you either, Farnsworth!"

31

Celia kept her steady gaze upon the gunfighter as she unfolded the napkin and spread it over her lap. Her first notion upon seeing Quinta sleeping off his drunk was to send him packing, for it was her opinion that a drunken gunfighter was worse than none at all. The way he'd stood up to her after she'd thrown that bucket of water at him, now the manner in which he was responding to her questions, told Celia that here was a man with backbone. But did Moses Quinta have enough grit to stand up to Talbot and his murdering bunch? And if he did agree to work for her, would he sell out to the cattle baron if he was offered more money? Loyalty was something, she'd found out, that you couldn't buy. Celia knew that the man seated in her husband's chair was her last chance to save the ranch. Suddenly it occurred to her that Quinta was the only man who'd graced her table since the death of Buck Farnsworth, the only man she'd ever loved, or would care for again. It had been cold and dreary when Buck had been laid to rest on a gentle knoll a short distance from the ranch site, with those who'd known him in attendance, other ranchers, hands who'd worked for them, some folks from Silver Springs, along with the preacher. Afterwards there'd been a time of withdrawal, of a grief so deep that for a time Celia felt she'd lose her mind. But it was the presence of her daughters that made Celia realize she had to go on living, take control of the ranch.

"Well, Mr. Quinta, shall we chow down?"

"I'd admire doing that." Reaching over with his fork, Quinta stabbed a steak off the platter. They ate silently from then on, speaking only to ask for some food, and with Moses Quinta's eyes drifting to the contents of this spacious house, thinking that the roots of this place went through topsoil to bedrock, he kind of envied the man who'd plant his boots permanentlike under this table. But living with a hellcat such as Celia Farnsworth could do more harm to a man than his climbing aboard a bronc which hadn't felt the touch of a saddle before, and with that sobering thought, Quinta stretched out his right arm to spear another steak.

"You are most definitely lacking in social graces, Mr. Quinta."

"That—" with his sleeve Quinta wiped a morsel of food away from his mouth—"so?"

"Around here the word 'please' carries a lot of weight."

He laid his fork down to speak around a mouthful of food. "Heard—heard a man say that once. Shot the hombre, anyways."

"You certainly have a way with words, too."

"Oh," said Quinta, "I ain't no great shakes as an orator the likes of Lincoln—or O.T. Shannon."

"O.T. Shannon?"

"Yup. Gent ran a house of pleasure down in Wichita. Sure was a spellbinder."

Celia said, "I'm sure you must have spent many evenings there."

"Being a gunfighter ain't all that much fun, ma'am. All I am is a restless wanderer. It won't be too much longer, I'm a-figuring, before there won't be any need for men like me. Why don't we cut out all this small talk and get to your reasons for sending me that letter."

"I believe that Carlton Talbot killed my husband."

"Can you prove that?"

"No more than I can prove it's going to rain tomorrow. The only proof I need is what Talbot's doing to the basin.

Others have suffered because of him."

"Heard that Talbot has a lot of bad habits."

"Sounds like you've crossed his path before, Quinta."

"Could have," he said quickly. "Though in my wanderings I sometimes get names and places twisted some."

"Or it could be, Mr. Quinta, all that whiskey you've consumed has something to do with your lack of memory."

"Reckon," Quinta said hotly, "you didn't ask me out here to discuss my morals—or other bad habits."

"Which you seem to have a lot of!"

The gunfighter's fork clattered onto his plate as he rose. "I recall you calling me a no-account gun runner too, ma'am."

"Why in hell—" Celia shoved up from her chair—"do you need all those guns?"

"I ain't heard, heard yet of a man getting killed with a T-bone steak—though this last one sure musta come from some old brindlehorn."

"Why, you damned tinhorn—"

"Ma'am, this here shouting ain't getting us no place. Sure, I knew Talbot before. He's the reason I spent time in prison. A long time ago we rode the owlhoot trail together. As for them rifles, I brung them along so's we'll have a fighting chance against all that firepower Talbot's men can throw against us."

Celia slumped back onto her chair, murmured, "So that big, bad cattle baron was an outlaw."

Easing down, Quinta said, "To tell you the truth, Talbot was no great shakes at it."

"I take it, Mr. Quinta, that I'm the only person you've told this to."

34

"There ain't no paper out on Talbot, if that's what you're driving at."

"Well, there'll be hell to pay when he finds out you're in the basin."

Moses Quinta related to the ranchwoman a few details about his being incarcerated in the territorial prison, and Celia told him of her desire to have him as her foreman.

"Someone who can handle a gun and men. I'll go under if I don't get my cattle to the railhead at Sheridan."

"Been up that way once. Seems to me the most logical way to get them there is south along the Bighorn River and around the Owl Creeks."

Celia refilled their cups. "That means bringing my hord onto Talbot land. The only other way is heading north into Montana and go around the Big Horns. But that could be a problem, at least from what a couple of hands told me when they passed through earlier this month. They've been working up at Matt Candry's Lazy M. Found out that Candry is fixing to sell out to the T-Bar. If that happens, Mr Quinta, Talbot will be able to seal off both routes leading out of the basin."

"There's always the Big Horns—"

"You mean, drive my cattle over them?"

"Reckon so."

"No!" That word came out before Celia could stop it. "Others, others have tried—and lost their herds."

"Well, it's something to chew over. How big a herd you figure on taking?"

"At the most, fifteen hundred. I'll keep the rest for breeding stock."

"That'll be a sizable chore, especially for four women—and me, if I hire on, that is. Mrs. Farnsworth, I'll be wanting two bucks a head for every steer that completes the drive, plus the usual foreman's wages."

"That's a little steep, Mr. Quinta."

"Seems you've got no other choice, ma'am."

"And seeing as how you're no gentleman, reckon it's a deal. Though there is one thing."

"That so?"

"Keep away from my daughters!"

"Why, ma'am, Moses Quinta here ain't no cradle robber. As for yourself, you're a mighty handsome woman—but with that nasty temper and all, that's another parcel of territory I ain't fixing on exploring either. Reckon I'll be a-saying goodnight now, because this old hoss sure needs his beauty sleep."

"Oh, Mr. Quinta, that you will. Our day starts at four o'clock sharp."

Moses Quinta groaned as he shoved up from the table, and after Celia Farnsworth followed him over and opened the door and he stepped outside, she said loudly, "Welcome to the working world, Quinta."

4

Three days after hiring on at the 77 Ranch Moses Quinta was heading for Silver Springs where he hoped to hire some men. He'd also discussed with Celia Farnsworth the need to get the smaller ranchers together, that by pooling their herds they stood a better chance of getting their cattle to Sheridan. Though Celia had expressed her doubts about this, Quinta's argument had been that all the other ranchers needed was for someone to take command.

The trail he followed brought him along the lower slopes of a mesa, where he drew rein and studied the flood plain of the Big Horn River opening up to him, the town of Silver Springs situated on a bluff where the river crooked toward the southeast, and on this side of it.

Along with some possibles and extra boxes of shells for his weapons, Quinta carried a pair of Civil War-vintage field glasses in his saddle bags, which he fished out and placed against his eyes. He focused the glasses in on the lower slopes of the bluff and with its houses, of log or unpainted board, with elm and cottonwood, and a few flickering poplars, casting down scattered remnants of shade. The lawns were more weed than grass, but there were a few lilac bushes. He glimpsed a woman through an upstairs window of one of the houses bare from the waist up before she slithered into dress that had a flowery pattern. Then he raised the glasses a notch to study Silver Springs' main thoroughfare, four blocks of hard-packed dirt without benefit of boardwalks.

First there was the town hall, whitewash peeling from it, a tattered flag hanging limply from a pole, and beyond that a loaded wagon such as homesteaders owned stood beside the livery stable. Three horses waited in front of the Ranchester Saloon; he could discern the T-Bar brand on the near horse. He bypassed a vacant lot until he came to the Antler Bar perched where the bluff curled down toward the river, with more horses tied before the saloon. On the opposite side of Main Street was a mercantile store, the land office, three vacant buildings and finally the Edgemont House, the largest building in town. A spur line of the Wyoming & Western railroad ran along the flat below the bluff, with Quinta learning on his only trip through here that a train came down once a week from Worland, which was more than enough, in his estimation. Silver Springs was a place that catered to the ranchers, and now that a lot of them were leaving, and some sodbusters, chances are that this town would shrivel up and die. Even now it had the look of a place that a heavy rainstorm could wash away.

"Yup, this place shows no more activity than a Kiowa village on a hot summer day," muttered Quinta as he rode on. But he was troubled by the presence of those T-Bar horses.

He used the better part of an hour to work his way over to the stagecoach road and follow it into town where he veered into an alley running behind the buildings on

Main Street. He'd heard tales about those kill-crazed punks with their pearl-handled guns and fancy outfits. They'd come riding brazenly down the main street of a strange town only to be back-shot and stripped of all their worldly possessions before being carted off to boothill. In one of them fanciful yarns wrote by some eastern writer who hadn't been further west than the Catskills, the hero, a handsome galoot with shoulders wide as Montana, cut down five desperadoes in a gunfight whilst being hit with an equal amount of slugs. The only thing was, Quinta knew from personal experience, that when a hunk of lead hit, it rendered flesh, slivered bones, and otherwise tore up a man something fierce. Then there was the numbing pain and delirium afterwards, if one lived, that is. So Quinta had a healthy respect for Mr. Colt or Remington, which was one of the reasons he'd outlived others of the same craft.

Dismounting behind the Antler Bar, he dusted himself off before passing through the back door and a hallway reeking of stale beer to pause when he came to the gaming room. He checked over those who were gambling, the bystanders, his view of a poker table bringing out the urge to sit in the game, and with some reluctance he continued on to the barroom.

Wedging a place at the back end of the long bar, he eased a spurred boot on the railing while waiting to be served. Those at the bar were talking in subdued manner, as of men about to attend a wake or who'd just received bad news of some sort. By their eyes, the way they stood, Quinta knew that the seeds of decay had set in. In the case of Silver Springs, he figured that the bad seed was rancher Charlton Talbot. But Quinta had little pity for men who didn't have the gumption to fight back. Now a barkeep moved away from the brass beerpulls to interrupt Quinta's musings.

"Quinta, wasn't it?"

He returned Sam Leone's smile. Leone had an empty sleeve pinned to the side of his waistcoat across the front of which a gold watch described a glittering arc. A veteran of the Indian Wars, Leone had been wounded at the battle of Terrapin Wells, and he was sallow of skin, with a receding hairline. Quinta had stopped here on his way up from Laramie, discovered then that Sam Leone had little use for Talbot or his hired guns.

"I didn't quite make it to Worland with them rifles."

Leone reached to the back bar for a bottle of Carstairs Best whiskey. "Heard you hired on at the 77 spread."

"News sure travels fast in these parts."

"And I reckon you're the reason some of Talbot's men have been loafing around town."

Quinta smiled over the rim of his shot glass. As the barkeep moved over to wait on another customer, Quinta glanced back at those seated around the tables in the barroom, which was separated from the gaming room by a low wall attached to studdings. The reason this place was so crowded, Quinta knew, was that Charlton Talbot had bought a seventy percent interest in the Ranchester Saloon, and though he'd let the same man run it, the prices had been raised considerable. The mercantile store, other business places, had suffered the same fate. It didn't take a blind man to figure out Talbot was trying to squeeze the town dry.

Sam Leone came back and flicked the towel he carried down at a fly. "Maybe you'd be interested in buying this place?"

"I cotton to larger towns. Tell me, are there any

40

ranchers in town?"

"Ben Tygee's over at that table talking to a home-steader name of Petrie."

"That wouldn't happen to be Petrie's wagon over at the livery stable?"

"Sorry to say it is. Petrie sold his place to the T-Bar. This keeps happening, Quinta, I won't have to worry about selling this place because Silver Springs'll be a ghost town."

Quinta bit the end from a cigar he'd pulled out of his pocket. "Mrs. Farnsworth spoke fondly of Tygee. Also that he's too stubborn to sell out—and maybe a little too old to be ranching."

"Don't tell Ben he's getting old, Quinta, or he might rope and hamstring you. Tygee's got a lot of pride."

"So's Celia Farnsworth," and saying that, Quinta downed the contents of his shot glass. "See you later." Placing a silver dollar on the bar, he picked up the bottle and shot glass with the other hand and began moving toward Ben Tygee's table.

Down among the border states the name Turk Oldham carried considerable weight, but up here in the Big Horn basin Oldham was just another hired gun working for the T-Bar spread. Though he'd killed a half-dozen men, two of them from ambush, his .44 Colt percussion wasn't notched. Oldham dressed plainly too, worn flat-crowned hat with the brim flopping over his eyes, faded Levi's and unadorned chaps. He was slender of build, with his stubbled face showing small, pimply scars left by smallpox, and like all men who lived as he did, his eyes were constantly shifting to check out others who were in

41

the Ranchester Saloon and movement outside. Unlike his two companions, who stood drinking with him at the bar, Oldham used the hand opposite his holstered gun to refill the shot glass or drink from it, or to scoop peanuts from a bowl on the worn bar top.

They'd been sent into town just in case some gunfighter calling himself Moses Quinta showed up, and after three days of this Oldham was getting tired of being in the presence of the other T-Bar hands. Why in hell, mused Oldham, didn't they just ride over to the 77 spread and kill the gunfighter? Part of Turk Oldham's problem was that he was looking to build up his reputation, and that those who rode with him held southern rawhiders, and that included Oldham, in contempt.

Oldham's eyes slid to Rye Moreland's swarthy face with its handlebar mustache and dark lines of brows above eyes red-rimmed from too much drinking. It rankled him that Moreland directed most of his remarks to Sid Aikens standing between them. It had been Moreland and him, reminisced Oldham, along with four others, who'd done the job on Buck Farnsworth up at Nowood Creek. What had happened there still left a bad taste in Oldham's mouth, the way Rye Moreland had shot the rancher Farnsworth in the back from damn near muzzle range after they'd disarmed the man. Even though Oldham had done his share of bushwhacking, those he'd gunned down had been armed, and he considered what Moreland had done out-and-out murder. Either Moreland didn't have any professional pride or, as Oldham suspected, the man was a coward. And he was getting a little weary of listening to Moreland brag as to how he would handle Moses Quinta if the man came to Silver Springs.

As Turk Oldham reached for the whiskey bottle, the batwings stirred and the marshal of Silver Springs came waddling toward the bar. The holstered Deane-Adams at Marshal Ike Ward's right hip seemed to be too small for a man of his bulk. He had no neck, only the large head covered by the greasy cattleman's hat sunk into sloping shoulders that were more fat than muscle. The black threads of the frock coat strained to cover a belly hanging over the gunbelt, and the shirt was more gray than white and had food and tobacco stains on it. Though he was clean-shaven, blue-black stubble showed in the places he'd missed. A confirmed bachelor, Ike Ward lived in a spare room over the harness shop, and those townspeople and ranchers who opposed Charlton Talbot's attempt to rule the basin considered the marshal Talbot's lapdog.

"Boys," Ward said as he scratched at an itch on his round face, "we've got ourselves a problem."

"You mean Quinta showed?"

The marshal told the barkeep to bring him a cold glass of beer as he looked at Rye Moreland. "Rye, you told me to keep an eye on that homesteader, Petrie. Been doing that. I just don't like the way Petrie's over to the Antler Bar and badmouthing the T-Bar—been drinking heavy, too."

"Can't you handle it?"

"Mr. Talbot said he didn't want any trouble here in town. Things are mighty unsettled now that a lot of folks are pulling up stakes and leaving. Maybe you boys could convince Petrie that he should leave town."

Moreland nudged Sid Aiken's shoulder. "Maybe this town needs to cheer it up is a good funeral."

"Now, boys, Mr. Talbot don't want no killings here."

"Damn, Marshal," lashed out Rye Moreland as he

43

spun and glared at the man, "what the hell do you think's gonna happen when Quinta shows?"

"Killing the sodbuster might rile folks up."

"Look, Oldham, you're paid to keep your mouth shut," said Moreland.

"As you say," Oldham said quietly. He knew Rye Moreland was itching for a fight, on the reckless edge of getting drunk. Now Oldham felt a twinge of disappointment when Moreland motioned for everyone to follow him.

Outside, Marshal Ike Ward blurted out, "Why, I'll just head over to the livery stable, boys, and harness up that homesteader's horses." Then he waddled away.

Sid Aikens spoke around the cigarette, "You sure are hell on wheels when it comes to law and order, Marshal." He and Moreland laughed together. "What you got in mind, Rye?"

"Well, I'll tell you, Aikens, I aim to do some rawhiding before we gun that damned sodbuster down."

"A piece of advice," said Turk Oldham.

"Which is something," said Moreland, "I don't want from you, Reb. Me and Sid, here, will go in the front. Oldham, cover us from the gaming room just in case this dumb sodbuster tries to make a break for it."

There were no street lamps, just the pale wedges of light seeping out of windows and doorways, along with a slice of lemon-colored moon hovering over the Owl Creek range. They waited until Oldham was out of sight, then Moreland and Aikens headed along the street accompanied by thin chink-chink of their spurs and toward the Antler Bar leaking yellow light and voices and piano music.

*   *   *

44

Curious eyes followed Moses Quinta over to the table pointed out to him by Sam Leone. At a glance he could tell that the homesteader had been drinking for some time. Cal Petrie had farmer's hands, the skin callused and work-worn, and a ruddy face scoured by the elements, the eyes in it full of resentment at this intrustion by Quinta. The younger man could only be Petrie's son, who had a .32 Remington thonged down so that it pressed against his left kidney, and who wore the working garb of a cowhand. Now it was the third man at the table who held Quinta's gaze in a steely one of its own. Ben Tygee's long face seemed to be hewed out of the heart of an oak; there were streaks of ashy-white hair in the graying mane. Tygee could be fifty, then again older, but the gray eyes belonged to a man who knew his place in life, and who could be tolerant of another's shortcomings. Over the Pendleton shirt Tygee had on a stockman's leather coat and string tie secured by a golden clasp, the gun he wore hidden under the flap. He acknowledged Quinta's presence with a quiet nod.

"Mr. Tygee, I'm Celia Farnsworth's new segundo."

Beckoning Quinta to pull up a chair, he drawled, "Heard you hired on out there, Mr. Quinta. This is Cal Petrie, his son, Tim."

Settling down to the rancher's left, Quinta set the bottle on the table and spoke to the homesteader, "Sorry to hear you're leaving."

"I ain't a bit sorry about it," Cal Petrie said bitterly. "And about half as sorry what Talbot'll be if I get within buckshot range. He done cheated me out of my place."

"Pa, you shouldn't—"

"Hush, boy, none of your lip now!"

Quinta smiled across the table at Tim Petrie, a slim-hipped youth of about twenty. "You figure on heading

45

back east?"

"Don't know," said the elder Petrie. "Most anywheres once I settle with that damned Talbot."

"That could be a sizable chore," said the rancher. "Could get you killed, Cal. Maybe it's time you considered your family."

"Don't need no sermonizing, Ben." He drained what whiskey there was in his glass, grabbed the bottle at his elbow to pour the glass full, the spillage trickling off the table and onto his dark blue coveralls.

"Ever do any blacksmithing?"

"Some."

"We could use a smitty out at the 77 spread."

"I've had my fill of ranches," the homesteader said sourly.

"Could you use another hand?"

"Boy, I told you to keep a lid on that mouth of yours. We're leaving this country for good."

"Need all the help we can get, Tim." Quinta relit his cigar. "Mr. Tygee, I suppose you heard that Celia Farnsworth is determined to get her herd to Sheridan."

"Celia's always been a forceful woman. But if anyone can do it, she can. She was always single-minded, about cattle or men. With that crew she's got, though, it could prove to be a chore."

"What if the other ranchers pooled their herds?"

Tygee rubbed his chin and squinted some before gazing back at Quinta. "That's a sensible notion, alright. But you've got to understand that some of the smaller ranchers out here are scared of what Talbot will do."

"And you, sir?"

Ben Tygee said gruffly, "Guess I'm getting too old to be scared—of what either man or nature can do anymore.

Though this rheumatism is giving me some concern." He forced a smile.

"It don't make no sense," spoke up the homesteader. "To bring all your cattle together just so's that damned Talbot can scatter them to hell and back. I say we organize a vigilante committee and go after that damned crook."

"I heard that, sodbuster!"

Moses Quinta and the others at the table glanced toward the batwings where the pair of hired guns stood. The wolfish grin on Sid Aikens' thin face widened when he saw the sudden glimmer of fear in the sodbuster's eyes. Aikens was a short man, maybe a couple of inches over five feet, but quick at the draw, and he knew it. Giggling, he flexed the fingers of his gun hand while glancing at Rye Moreland, who swayed some where he stood with his legs spread apart, one hand hooked in his gun belt. Moreland was bigger than most of the men here in the saloon, and bare knuckles was his specialty, but he'd primed himself to kill someone. He'd seen the rancher, Tygee, around town, but the stranger sitting there struck a responsive chord in Moreland's mind, and he spoke to Aikens out of the corner of his mouth. "Know him?"

"Can't be too good with them guns he's wearing," Aikens said cockily, "if he's keeping a damned sodbuster company. Let's take them." He giggled again, savoring what was to come.

"That rotgut sure gives you courage, farmer! Enough so that one of your friends can lend you a gun!"

"Easy," said Tygee, placing a firm hand on the homesteader's arm.

"I'm waiting, farmer! No damned sodbuster is gonna

badmouth my boss and get away with it!"

Back in the gaming room, Turk Oldham had stationed himself by the roulette table to watch the play while waiting for the others to come into the bar. Through the latticework partition separating this room from the front barroom he could see the heads of those seated at the tables, the sudden commotion as they shoved up from their tables to move out of the way. Coming around the roulette table, Oldham stopped when he had a clear view of the homesteader's table. Now Oldham's hand dropped near his gun butt when the big man seated there announced that he was the gunfighter Moses Quinta. This was going to work out better than Oldham had anticipated. Moreland and Aikens were liquored up, and for certain Quinta would gun them down. Then all Oldham had to do was draw on the gunfighter and he wouldn't have to split the bounty money the rancher had put on Quinta with the others. "Come on," Oldham muttered impatiently, "show us how good you are, Moreland."

Then Turk Oldham stiffened as something hard was pressed against his back, while a raspy voice said, "Best leave that iron where it is." And the hired gun did just that when the man holding the antiquated Dragoon pistol reached under Oldham's backsides to bring the point of the Green River knife jabbing into his testicles, and with Turk Oldham sort of easing the heels of his boots up from the sawdust-covered floor.

"Count me out," Oldham gasped.

"Mighty pleased to hear that," said Zach Lankford around a satisfied cackle, giving his knife a little nudge that brought the hired gun up a little higher. Lankford, the last of an original breed called a plainsman, had been hanging around town too, and overheard the T-Bar hands telling what they were going to do to Moses Quinta over at the Ranchester Saloon. When Quinta had walked through the gaming room, Lankford had recognized the gunfighter from a picture he'd seen in a newspaper, and though it wasn't Zach Lankford's way to mix in other's business, he figured three against one was a little unfair, especially since this one here had it in mind to shoot the gunfighter in the back. Lankford wore buckskins, the graying beard coming down over his fringed shirt, and he was blocky, with black eyes sunk into their sockets.

"Quinta, you don't look so tough to me!" came Rye Moreland's voice.

"Tough has nothing to do with it," replied Quinta. "Just who can shoot straighter."

It was then that the homesteader made a grab for one of Quinta's holstered guns, and as Quinta reacted by shoving the man away, Rye Moreland drew, a slug from his weapon slamming into the table where Quinta was standing.

Quinta's guns blurred out of their holsters, bucking as he shot Moreland in the chest, with Sid Aikens taking a slug alongside his nose. Aikens managed to pull the trigger, but the report of his weapon came into dead ears, the hired gun's body coming unhinged and toppling to the floor. The gun in Quinta's left hand spurted flame again, striking Moreland in the stomach where he still stood trying to bring his gun to bear on Quinta, the shock of what was happening registering in his gaping eyes. Moreland swung sideways and stumbled against the batwings, reached vainly to hold himself erect as the weapon became too heavy to hold and he dropped it, then reeled to fall outside.

"Here's another one!" exclaimed Zach Lankford as he shoved Turk Oldham away.

Spinning that way, Moses Quinta held his fire when he saw that the other T-Bar hand had raised his arms, and with Oldham saying, "Got no quarrel with you, Quinta." Even on his best day Oldham knew he was no match for the gunfighter, knew that by drawing he'd die like the others, and the thought cut deep into his pride.

"You've got a gun," Quinta said tauntingly as he leathered his Colts. "Go for it!"

There were muffled chortles of laughter as the hired gun began backing away. Oldham threw the plainsman an I'll-see-you-later look, before hurrying out the way he'd come in.

Now that the sound of gunfire was stilled, patrons of the Antler Bar began gathering around the bodies. At the table where Quinta stood, the homesteader said shakily, "Guess it's time I left the basin. Let's go, boy." And they left after Cal Petrie had said his goodbyes to the rancher, Tygee.

"Think he'll go after Talbot?"

"I doubt it," said Quinta. "I reckon now Petrie realizes he'd be signing his death warrant if he did. Could you set up a meeting with the other ranchers? It won't do any harm to tell them my ideas on pooling their herds."

"Guess it won't at that. One thing, Mr. Quinta, from now on you'll be a marked man in the basin. Talbot isn't the kind to let something like this go unanswered. But I'll throw in with the 77 spread when the time comes to make that drive to Sheridan." They shook hands, then Tygee left the saloon.

"Listen up!" said Quinta, waiting until he'd gotten everyone's attention. "I'm Quinta, the new foreman out at the 77. I need men who know something about cattle. Forty a month and found." The expressions on the faces of those listening to Quinta were guarded, as of men who were judging Moses Quinta for what he'd just done to the hired guns, and maybe the same thing could happen to them if they went against the T-Bar bunch. One by one they turned away, either to pick up their drinking or gambling or to leave, and though Quinta was disappointed, in a way he didn't blame them for not hiring on.

"Seems these folks are looking more for a position than work."

Quinta turned and returned Zach Lankford's gap-toothed smile, and then said, "I sure appreciate what you did."

"Name's Lankford, Zach to my friends, most of whom have gone under now. Been wintering in the Absarokas—stringing trap lines and such. Your offer's mighty interesting, Quinta, but I sure enough hate longhorns."

"You ever work on a ranch before, Mr. Lankford?"

"Call me Zach, damnit," he said pleasantly. "Nope. Playing nursemaid to hoofed critters ain't my game."

"Can you cook?"

"Sure can!" bristled the plainsman. "Been batching all my natural life."

"Well, I need one."

"Hmmm, it's a fact this here child needs a grubstake. You know, Quinta, I like your style. So you've got yourself a cook."

"Maybe we should drink to that."

"Grizzly bears couldn't keep me away from that offer."

When Moses Quinta left Silver Springs the following morning it was with Zach Lankford riding alongside on his Indian cayuse and the sun just clearing the Big Horns.

51

The bellies of a line of clouds to the northwest were black with rain, and the wind gusting before it sent a few dust devils scurrying across the prairie. Just after the shooting at the Antler Bar, the marshal of Silver Springs had put in an appearance, and was all for arresting Quinta, but the townspeople, much to Quinta's surprise, had backed up his story that it was self-defense. Zach Lankford's presence had helped too, especially after the plainsman had told the marshal in no uncertain words that he'd better believe what he'd been told or his scalplock would be dangling from Lankford's belt.

Another surprise awaited Moses Quinta when he left the stagecoach road and reached the elevation where he'd used his field glasses to study the town of Silver Springs in the form of a man squatting beside his horse and in shadow cast by the mesa. As Quinta and the plainsman pulled up, Tim Petrie came erect and said uncertainly, "I'd like to work for you, Mr. Quinta."

"Where's your pa?"

"Heading out of the basin. But like I told Pa, I've got to lead my own life."

"That's good enough for me, Tim. But there could be gunplay."

"I figured that's included in the forty a month and found."

Cackling, Lankford said, "You sure you're the offspring of a homesteader?"

Quinta, around a smile, said, "Well, guess we'll find that out, won't we? Let's ride. We've got a lot of cattle to gather."

5

The horseman trailing a pair of saddled horses was halfway across the alkali flats before some of the men gathered around a pole corral noticed the plume of dust. Slowly they swung out their attention from the big roan trying to scrape its rider against the poles of the corral to the north. Strangers had a way of finding their way out here to the T-Bar, though those living in the basin rarely ventured here. And if it was a lawman, it would be the marshal of Silver Springs, who reported to the rancher Talbot about twice a week.

Bill Liscomb, a rawboned waddy coming onto his thirties, had been standing off by himself near a wood pile while watching the action in the corral, one spurred boot propped on a hunk of cottonwood, the dislike he felt for the hired guns gathered around the corral gleaming in his eyes. One of Talbot's ramrods, Liscomb was in charge of the working hands, while the other ramrod, Tex Whitney, bossed the hired guns. All of Liscomb's men were out on the vast reaches of the ranch, and he'd come back for some supplies, would head out once the day became a little cooler. Sometimes Bill Liscomb had it in mind to quit, but there was his family in Silver Springs to consider; even so, Charlton Talbot's reckless and bloodthirsty ways were a reflection, Liscomb knew, on him and those he supervised.

Now in the afternoon haze he could make out Turk Oldham astride his gray bronc, and unlike the others, Bill Liscomb stayed put as the hired guns detached themselves from the corral and moved in a group toward the road coming down from the north and up to a low stone wall.

Turk Oldham came in at a lope and through the open gate where he reined up. Removing his dusty hat, Oldham wiped the caked sweat from his brow. Then someone asked, "Where's Moreland and Aikens?"

"Ran into Moses Quinta," he told them.

"He killed both of them?"

"They was drunk," he said, dropping the reins of the other horses before touching spurs to his gray.

The lane carried Oldham through a stand of cottonwoods and aspens and over a log bridge spanning a narrow creek meandering off toward the Big Horn River, some five miles to the west. The creek separated the main house from the other buildings. The house Oldham was riding toward had an outer courtyard, a red tiled roof, whitewashed adobe walls. A guard came out to intercept Oldham when he reached the arched entryway.

"This better be good, Oldham."

Swinging to the ground, the hired gun said flatly, "I figure Mr. Talbot would like to hear how Moses Quinta took care of Moreland and Aikens."

"Wait here." The guard hurried back into the courtyard, only to appear several minutes later accompanied by Whitney, the ramrod, a lanky man wearing one gun, a Colt .45, who told Oldham that Charlton Talbot would see him.

Inside the courtyard, Oldham trailed behind the ramrod as they went along a tiled walkway to an open side door. Motioning Oldham to go inside, the ramrod came in after the hired gun. The rancher was seated in an overstuffed chair covered with tanned cowhide. At Talbot's left hand was a small table on which reposed several bottles of liquor; a gold-headed cane leaned against the chair on the other side. The room was small, almost barren of furnishings except for rifles stacked in a gun rack and the black maw of the fireplace.

Charlton Talbot had the look of a man who'd settled into himself, of someone growing old before his time, and hating it. He'd put on too much weight, and it showed in the puffy facial skin and sagging jawline. Though there were prominent sacks under the watery blue eyes, cynical arrogance flashed out of them as he stared at the hired gun, Oldham. The black hair had been trimmed that morning by his valet, a mandarin, the only other servant in the large house being the cook, a Mexican woman, who kept within the confines of her kitchen or cleaned the house when Talbot was away from the ranch.

Reaching for his glass, Talbot sipped at the brandy, then in his hard Southern drawl he said, "Tell me in detail just what happened."

"Well, Mr. Talbot," began Oldham, "Quinta came into town alright. Was boozing it up over at the Antler Bar. Which was where he gunned down the others."

"Where were you when this happened?"

"Outside," Oldham lied. "Moreland said he and Aikens could handle it."

"Obviously you can't tell me if this gunfighter is as good as they say he is."

55

Under the damning scrutiny of the ramrod and Charlton Talbot, the hired gun knew he'd made a tactical error. It was too late now to tell the truth of what happened back there, and any hopes Oldham had of currying the rancher's favor had vanished. The tension left him when Tex Whitney spoke up.

"Now that Quinta's working for the 77 spread, that should tie these killings in with your plans to buy the place. We've got the law at Silver Springs on our side. I say to hell with public opinion. My boys are ready to ride."

"No!" Talbot exploded. "Everyone out!"

Only after these hard-eyed men were gone did Charlton Talbot throw his glass down to have it shatter on the floor. He realized that Whitney, like the others, was probing for his weaknesses, but underneath the outward signs of decay Talbot knew he was a lot tougher than those who'd hired their guns out to him. They killed for pay, and probably the pure enjoyment of it; Charlton Talbot for a reason. This was what separated men who ran with the pack from those with brains and the cunning to use them. But Talbot had to admit that he'd panicked when Marshal Ike Ward had told him of Moses Quinta's presence in the basin.

He'd first seen Celia Farnsworth at a dance held at the Cimarron Hotel in Worland, felt instantly the need to possess such a beautiful woman. Her refusal to dance with him had ony inflamed passions he'd managed to hold in check while he went about the business of building up his cattle empire. True, there were women he kept, but merely chattel possessions, giving him what he wanted for coin of the realm. Celia Farnsworth was too proud and headstrong for her own good, and in order to

56

acquire such a woman, Talbot knew that he'd have to break her first, which to him meant her losing the 77 spread. Respect for him, and love, if that were possible, would come after she'd become his wife. His fear was that if he sent his hired guns out there after Quinta, Celia or one of her daughters might be harmed. But sooner or later, he believed, an opportunity would present itself in which Quinta would be taken care of. As for Celia, Talbot knew of the note the bank over at Worland was holding on her ranch, that it was due at the end of this year, so all he had to do was to block any attempts by Celia to get her herd to market.

"Pride goeth before a fall," he said, while grasping his cane and pushing up from the chair. The limp was a result of Talbot's being thrown from his horse, the fall onto rocky terrain shattering his left leg. The bones hadn't settled properly, having been set by a local doctor; once things had settled down in the basin he planned to go to a specialist in Denver.

He limped down a hallway until he came to a door on his right, which he unlocked. He let himself into a square room dominated by a large rectangular table and a thronelike chair with his brand embossed into its high back. Locking the door, he went over and lifted himself into the chair and settled his elbows on the armrests. Into Charlton Talbot's eyes came a glimmer of smugness as he gazed upon a cartographical mockup of the Big Horn basin spread over the table. It showed in miniature relief the streams, rivers and surrounding mountains. The boundaries of every ranch in the basin were marked in various colors, Talbot's T-Bar and the others he'd acquired in royal blue, those ranchers opposed to him in scarlet, the handful of others in green. There were also the towns—Silver Springs, Cody, Greybull, Worland. The basin was in the shape of a Charbanet wine bottle: a wide bottom to the south, with the sides tapering outward to run into a long bottleneck at its northern extremity, a tract of land blessed with water and prairie grass some 90 miles wide, 150 from north to south. Talbot likened it to the valley of the Mormons over in Utah, and like that religious sect, this was going to be his empire. Already men had died by his orders, more would have to die in order to make his dream a reality.

From one of his working hands, Raoul Dixon, who was sparking one of Celia Farnsworth's daughters, he'd found out about the letter Celia had written to Moses Quinta. That Quinta was still alive had come as a surprise to the rancher, who had figured that by now the gunfighter's wild ways had either seen him gunned down by one of his kind or rotting away in some prison. And even if Quinta did tell the ranchwoman that Talbot had once ridden the outlaw trail, it would be the word of a respected rancher against a gunfighter's. Talbot had used his influence to get Quinta arrested on a trumped-up charge and sent to the territorial prison at Laramie, and the man's unexpected release had come as another surprise. The fact that Quinta could have important friends in the territory added fuel to Talbot's worries. So he must have eyes out at the 77, and that meant Raoul Dixon.

Talbot locked the door after leaving the room and made his way to the front door where he found his ramrod out in the inner courtyard talking to one of the guards, and curtly the rancher summoned Tex Whitney to him. Then Talbot brought the ramrod back inside and to a south wing of the house where his office was located. "First of all, I want Raoul Dixon brought here."

"I'll send someone after Dixon."

"And there's the matter of the Lazy M." Talbot picked up one of two envelopes lying on his cluttered desk. "Give this to the land agent at Worland; in turn, he'll give you a deed made out for the Lazy M. This other envelope contains what money Matt Candry will be getting for his place."

"Candry's a stubborn fool, Mr. Talbot. He wouldn't have nothing to do with us last time we were there. Ran us off at gunpoint."

"This time you'll take enough men to do the job right."

"Meaning?"

"Either Candry sells—or he dies!"

6

A cloud shadow passed over the Farnsworth women where they were gathered just outside a line shack tucked up along the northern reaches of the 77 spread, with all of them staring southwesterly at the approaching riders. They weren't alarmed, since the keen-eyed Beth Farnsworth had recognized Moses Quinta's horse, though even she couldn't see who the others were due to the afternoon sun being in back of them.

The line shack was located in that high rolling country where the fringes of the prairie reached to the foothills rising toward the blood-and-ocher-colored cliffs of the Big Horns. There were no fence lines to distinguish the limits of the 77 Ranch, only the creek's common boundary lines known to those who owned the land. In the nearby pole corral their saddled horses waited patiently, with the "camp stump," really the bony-sheen stump of a tree rising to a height of about four feet to jagged ends of burnt wood where lightning had struck it. There could be found a shovel and crosscut saw leaning against it, a fishing creel stuck on a protruding knob of wood, the single-bladed axe stuck into a lower section of stump that had been sawed level.

While they waited, Celia Farnsworth looked to the west to see if the cattle they'd gathered that day had started to drift, a bunch of around fifty longhorns and white faces. Thoughts of leaving this high country if she lost the ranch rode constantly with Celia during these long working days. She felt there was no grander place that this windswept prairie with its sagebrush, cactus and spangled wildflowers blooming in the spring, where rawboned mesas looked down upon rugged arroyos, the jagged peaks stacked up on all sides of the basin, where a Chinook would suddenly sweep down to warm up those chilling days of wintry January, or where a person could take in air cleansed by a summer thunderstorm. Even the game animals—elk, pronghorns, mule and white-tailed deer—could sense that this was an unshackled place. But it wouldn't be if Charlton Talbot had his way, and anger caused Celia to dump the remaining coffee out of her tin cup.

"It's Tim!" shouted Amanda, breaking away from the line shack in a run that carried her toward the riders.

"Tim Petrie?" Celia said wonderingly. She stood there while her other daughters trailed at a walk after Amanda.

Quinta laughed at the crimson staining Tim Petrie's face when the girl reached them and said, "Oh, Tim, I thought . . . you'd gone." And when Tim stopped to climb out of the saddle, Quinta and Zach Lankford rode on toward the line shack, with Beth and Sara gazing curiously at the plainsman, who doffed his hat at them in passing.

Drawing up by the pole corral, Quinta dismounted and moved over to a water bag hanging near the line shack door while trying to gauge the ranchwoman's thoughts. Before drinking, he said, "Got you a cook, ma'am."

"Yup, you can just call me Zach," he said around the wad of tobacco bulging out one cheek.

"Howdy . . . Zach," she said uncertainly. "Quinta, I want a word with you."

"Sure."

"In private, if you don't mind." Celia entered the shack, with Moses Quinta coming in behind, and she added, "I sent you to Silver Springs to hire some hands. And all you can bring me is a cook and a . . . a kid."

"On the way up from Silver Springs Zach Lankford was sure bragging on his cooking. Petrie's old enough to be of some use, too."

"That . . . Lankford person is—"

"He calls himself a plainsman."

"Great," exclaimed Celia as she placed her hands on her hips. "My foreman brings me a moonstruck plainsman—along with a lovestruck kid. Which will only make getting to Sheridan with my herd that much tougher."

"The situation you're in," came back Quinta, "you shouldn't be too choosy."

"For a foreman, you're mighty uppity!"

"Done what I could over in Silver Springs." He stepped to the stove and picked up the coffeepot, looked about for a cup. "Trouble is, everyone's scared of Talbot's men. And speaking of them, I had a little ruckus."

"Such as?" said Celia as she tossed him a cup.

"Killing two of Talbot's hired guns."

Celia considered this as she strode to the door and gazed outside for a few moments, but her face was set when she swung back to Quinta. "I should be sorry for those men, but I'm not. Quinta, it's coming onto August.

63

We've got a month, maybe less, to gather my herd, because winter has a way of setting in early in these parts."

Nodding, he said, "Ran into Ben Tygee. He goes along with pooling our herds. I sold him on the idea of getting the other ranchers together in Silver Springs to discuss this. Tygee'll let us know when the meeting's set."

"Having it in Silver Springs could be dangerous, Quinta. If word gets out, that Talbot bunch is certain to show up."

"Maybe you're right. Somehow Talbot's men knew I was working here."

Celia frowned. "But you've only been here about a week."

"Could be that Charlton Talbot found out about that letter you sent me."

"Could be," she said thoughtfully. "Well, Quinta, there's still a lot of daylight left—and we've got cattle to round up."

"Coming," he muttered hastily as he drained his cup, then followed Celia outside and over to the pole corral, with Celia telling everyone to mount up. Leading her horse out of the corral, she gazed up at Tim Petrie waiting aboard his horse. "Young man, I'll take a chance that you know something about cattle."

"Ma'am, Mrs. Farnsworth, I've done some ranch work before."

"I'll be the judge of what I'm going to pay you. Where are your folks?"

"Last I seen of them they was heading south out of Silver Springs."

"And, Quinta," called Celia, "it might be a good idea to leave your bedroll behind." This rejoinder brought smiles from her daughters. "Alright, we've been working those draws over yonder. Now we'll head more to the south. Petrie, you'll pair up with me; Beth and Sara; Quinta, you and Amanda."

Zach Lankford peered over at the ranchwoman when he'd led his horse out of the corral and was untying his bedroll. "This means I've got to work alone?"

"It does," said Celia, "since you claim to be a cook. It'll be mighty nice tasting someone else's cooking for a change. But if I find you've been lying to me, Lankford, come morning you can ride out." Then Celia Farnsworth spurred away from the line shack, settling her horse into a fast canter as the others fanned out behind.

By moonlight, and under a glittering canopy of stars, they came riding back to the line shack, the cattle they'd gathered mingling with the others. The other horses in the pole corral nickered and milled about, but settled down after a while. In thoughtful silence Mooce Quinta unsaddled his horse while eying Celia's daughters, knowing that the daily grind of long hours spent in the saddle was wearing them down. Before too much longer, he knew they would need more help. He turned his horse loose to watch it go with the others a short distance to a creek meandering through a marshy area, the dark gleam of water in a wider spot revealing a beaver dam. Then he moved wearily with the others toward light playing over the log step in front of the line shack and spilling yellowly onto the hard-packed ground. Zach Lankford came to stand in the doorway, wiping his hands on the towel wrapped around his waist.

"Was wondering when you folks would show," he

said. "But the grits is ready."

Quinta glanced at Celia and said hopefully, "He sure sounds like a cook."

"Whatever he managed to throw together doesn't smell too bad either," she commented dryly.

On the bench beside the door, window light beaming upon it, there was a wash basin and a pail of water with a dipper in it, a square bar of soap, a towel hanging from a wall peg. The younger women washed up first, and when it was her turn, Celia threw over her shoulder, "I expect you gentlemen to avail yourselves of water."

"Expected to," responded Quinta, and turning to Tim Petrie, he muttered, "This henpecking can get on a man's nerves. Yup, she's a hard woman to please."

"What was that?"

"I said, ma'am, all this riding sure enough brings out the hunger in a man."

When the business of washing was over, the men lined up behind the Farnsworth women as Zach Lankford ladled beef stew onto their plates from the big enamel pot on the cast-iron stove. Celia and her daughters settled down at the small table. After they'd helped themselves to sourdough biscuits and scooped greens onto their plate, Quinta and Tim moved outside and sat down on the front step. One tentative mouthful by Celia told her that she had a cook on her payroll, and she glanced at Lankford hovering anxiously over by the stove.

"This isn't too bad . . . Zach," she said. "But I'll reserve judgment until I've sampled more of your cooking."

"Ma," said Beth, "this is better than your beef stew."

"Yeah," piped up Sara, "I like it too," and through a

giggle she added, "But Mr. Lankford sure dresses funny."

"Missy," said Lankford as he stroked at his beard, "reckon I'm getting to old to wear civilized clothes. But you don't judge a man by what he wears—" he jabbed a finger at his heart—"only what he feels here."

"I—I was just funning, Mr. Lankford."

"That's alright, Sara girl. A person can't stand a little joshing, well, he ain't long for this world. Now, there's more stew over here; got some more biscuits popping in the oven. If'n I had some apples, why I could make you the best doggone pie you ever sunk your choppers in."

When supper was over, Celia's daughters went into the only bedroom and closed the door, and Celia moved over to stand in the doorway and say to Tim Petrie, "With a little work you just might be a cowhand."

"Appreciate that, Mrs. Farnsworth."

"Ma'am," said Quinta around his cigar, "your daughters are getting worn out."

"I know, and it worries me."

"Could be I could find some help up at Worland. Another thing, that store in Silver Springs has raised its prices considerable."

"Because of Talbot," she said grimly. "In another day or two we'll bring these cattle back to the ranch. You and Lankford can take the supply wagon and head up there. OK, you boys will have to bed down out here." Entering the line shack, she lifted the lamp off the table, then paused to gaze at Lankford, who was picking up his bedroll. "Zach, I'm pleased you hired on." Without waiting for his response, she went into the bedroom and closed the door.

67

They spread their bedrolls on the eastern side of the line shack and away from the pole corral, then brought their saddles over to use as pillows. From his saddlebag Quinta took out a bottle of whiskey and sat down on his bedroll, while Lankford eased down Injun-fashion and eyed the bottle as he fished a silver-plated harmonica out of a shirt pocket. Beyond Quinta, Tim Petrie had snuggled into his bedroll.

"You know, boys," said the plainsman, "a man sort of gets used to going it alone out here, gets kind of spooked when others are around—not that I mind the present company. Many's a time—" he nodded at the black hulks of the Big Horns showing patches of snow on their higher reaches—"that I camped up there." Quinta passed him the bottle and Lankford drank from it before handing it to Tim Petrie, who waved it away and said, "I don't drink."

"In that case, you'll never get hair on your chest," remarked Quinta, claiming the bottle again. "Tell me, Zach, what's the chances of driving a herd over the Big Horns to Sheridan?"

The gap-toothed smile showing, he said, "Over the Big Horns? Slim at best, I'd say. Why?"

"Just that we might have to. Celia tells me that Talbot wants to buy the Lazy M, which is located up north where the basin narrows. And if he does buy it, he sure as sin won't let us pass across his land. Nor to the south either, I'm figuring."

"There might be a way, Quinta. But I'd have to scout it out. Place called Granite Pass. But drive a herd up them peaks. Looka there, boys, that's Cloud Peak, darn near fourteen thousand feet high, according to some army surveyor I ran into, then there's Mather Peak, Hazelton, barriers reaching near to the stars." Easing into his bedroll, Lankford struck a tune on his harmonica, a mournful ballad Quinta recognized as having originated with the nomadic Blackfeet.

"Glad to have you with us, Zach; you too, Tim. And, Zach, before you doze off put a do-not-disturb sign on the door."

The plainsman stopped to cackle for a couple of seconds before swinging into another tune on his harmonica, and as Moses Quinta stretched out in his bedroll and pulled the hat over his eyes, it was not the dreamless sleeps of the past that filled his mind, rather thoughts and images of this new life, and surprisingly enough, scattered thoughts of the ranchwoman, Celia Farnsworth.

7

Beth Farnsworth slapped the ends of the reins against her gloved hand as she looked at the cattle grazing on the flats near the ranch site. Two days ago they'd brought back more cattle, and she was grateful for the sanctuary of her own bed, a few days' respite until they headed out again.

In her was a yearning to see Raoul Dixon, and she envied Amanda riding alongside Tim Petrie on the fringes of the herd. Ever since Tim had come here, there'd been a new sparkle in Amanda's eyes, of a love rekindling between her and someone she believed had left the basin.

"You're torturing yourself," Beth murmured, and with a tug at the reins brought the pinto around where she gazed at a distant bluff overlooking the Big Horn River. It was from this point that Raoul Dixon would use a piece of mirror to signal his presence, and for the past two days her eyes had been constantly going there during the late afternoon hours. Without question, Beth knew that she loved Raoul, and it was her desire that he quit working for the T-Bar, for in the company of those hired guns he could change or get hurt.

Now the longing in her heart to see Raoul Dixon again caused Beth to spur her pinto to the southwest and away from the herd ground and to hold her horse at a slow lope until a ravine brought her out of eyesight. Now she went at a run along the ravine floor, and brought the pinto up a cut and onto the prairie, the shadows they cast elongating away. Then, to her surprise, a reflecting beam of light came from the bluff, and bursting out of Beth Farnsworth was a laugh of pure joy. "Raoul, I knew you'd come."

Another mile of hard riding carried her below the bluff and onto the flood plain which was narrower at this point than further south, and down to her rendezvous point on the river bank. Lithely she dismounted, tied the reins to the branch of a willow tree, and then Raoul Dixon was there, riding slowly along the bank and up to Beth Farnsworth. Almost before he could get off his horse she was in his arms.

"Raoul, Raoul—how I've missed you." Their kiss was more tender than passionate, as if both of them sensed hard and dangerous times were coming. He left his horse there, and with his arm around Beth's waist, they slipped up the bank and settled down in a little grassy cul-de-sac shaded by cottonwoods.

Raoul Dixon had inherited the soft brown eyes and black hair of his Mexican mother, and the rugged handsome looks of his father, a former Jayhawker out of Kansas who'd abandoned both Raoul and his mother years ago. Removing the flat-crowned hat, he tossed it aside and took her in his arms. "Once again, my lovely, I'm asking you to marry me."

Beth said sadly, "Not as long as you're working for the T-Bar, Raoul. If you quit there, we—we could leave the basin."

"You mean you'd leave your family?" questioned Raoul in his accented voice.

"If it meant keeping you, yes."

"Your mother, I guess she still doesn't like my seeing you?"

"That she hasn't changed her mind about. Raoul, I was wondering, did you—did you tell anyone about that letter Mother sent to Moses Quinta?"

"Well, *si,* a couple of hands."

"It doesn't matter now, I suppose. Sooner or later Talbot would have found out about our taking on Quinta." Then she sensed that something was troubling Raoul Dixon, and added, "You're holding something back, aren't you?"

There was a flare of hostility in his eyes, but he blinked it away and plucked out a blade of grass. Finally, he said, "There is. I didn't come here on my own this time. Talbot sent me."

"Why?"

"Beth, I'm supposed to find out if the 77 is getting a herd together."

"Of course, Raoul, we need to sell some cattle."

"Also, when and by what route you plan to drive them to Sheridan." With an angry gesture he threw away the blade of grass. "Talbot is a cruel man. Ambitious and cruel. The way he talks about your mother, I—I think he has strong feelings for her."

A mocking laugh came from Beth as she rose. "Mother would just love to hear that. Do you enjoy spying for Talbot?"

Pushing up from the ground, he grasped her arms. "Listen to me, I would have told you none of this if I was

73

spying for Talbot. When I go back I shall tell Señor Talbot what he wants to hear."

"And just what is that?"

"That you are having trouble getting your herd together—because you don't have enough help."

"But that we do plan to go to Sheridan?"

"But of course, Beth, otherwise Talbot won't believe me."

"This might work to our advantage," she said thoughtfully.

"Señor Talbot wants me to report back to him right away. Then I am to come back here and tell your mother that I no longer work for Señor Talbot. Could you stand to have me around every day, my life?"

"Oh, Raoul, every . . . every day." Arm in arm they moved down the bank and over to their horses. "Be careful, Raoul, when you talk to Talbot."

"I shall be most humble," he said around a smile. "But lie like I've never lied before." Now they clung desperately to one another, until Raoul broke away and swung aboard his horse. He gazed down upon Beth Farnsworth for a few moments, then wheeled his horse around to let it canter southward along the east bank of the Big Horn River.

As he rode, Raoul Dixon mulled over in his mind just what he'd say to the rancher. Though he knew that sooner or later Talbot would send his hired guns against the 77 spread, he hadn't mentioned this to Beth Farnsworth. This news, he felt, would only be another burden the woman he loved would have to carry around.

Shock filtered into his eyes when the familiar sound of a shell being levered into a rifle came from the brush lining the bank along which he rode.

"Don't make any sudden moves!" The brush parted and Moses Quinta revealed himself seated in the saddle of his horse, the rifle pointing at Dixon resting on the pommel. "What's your game, Dixon?"

Carefully Raoul Dixon raised his arms before saying, "You—you must be the gunfighter, Quinta."

"I'm Quinta, alright. I do appreciate your telling Talbot about that letter Mrs. Farnsworth sent to me."

"All I did, Señor Quinta, was mention it to some of the hands."

"Now, as to why you're sneaking around here, Dixon, I want—"

"It is true that I and Beth have been meeting down here." Then Raoul Dixon narrated to the gunfighter what he'd just told Beth Farnsworth. "So you see, I am only protecting the interests of the 77 spread. I love Beth, and—and she loves me."

"You've got a pretty persuasive argument, alright. Go back and report to Talbot. But when you come back, I ain't too certain that Mrs. Farnsworth will take you on, Dixon. Though it's sure worth a try. I do hope, too, that you ain't lying to me about all of this."

"I swear, Señor Quinta, on the grave of my mother!"

"Well, Dixon, when you get back there be damned convincing what you tell Charlton Talbot or he'll be swearing over your grave. *Adios,* kid." Quinta swung his horse around and was gone.

8

Worland was a bigger town than its counterpart further south along the Big Horn River, having a couple of dance halls, one theater and several saloons, one of them being the Broadaxe Bar, on a side street just around the corner from Main Street. One notable feature of this saloon was the collection of axes lining the walls, the other being a sort of community bulletin board run by the owner, the reason Moses Quinta and Zach Lankford were angling across the street, pausing to let a wagon rumble by before stepping onto the boardwalk and entering.

They'd started out well before daybreak in the supply wagon, with Quinta mostly grumbling about the rough ride, the plainsman enjoying himself while pointing out various places he'd been in the Big Horns, and both of them being forced to drink water because Quinta's stock of whiskey had been depleted. Upon arriving in Worland, the wagon had been left at Tanner's General Store along with a list of those supplies they wanted.

"Been saving this double eagle piece for a special occasion," stated Zach Lankford as he commandeered a table. "Barkeep, just keep that cold beer and whiskey coming until this money is used up. Some of them hard-boiled eggs and pickled pigs' feet will set me up fine, too." After saying all of that, Lankford draped his hat on an empty chair and eased onto another one as he swatted at an errant fly. Quinta sagged gingerly onto a chair across the table.

"That buggy seat is torture to a riding man," he growled.

"Where you gents from?" inquired the barkeep upon arriving at the table bearing a couple of trays, the beer steins and whiskey bottle on one, the shot glasses and the food Lankford had ordered on the other. He set both trays down and palmed the double eagle piece.

"You ever hear of the 77 spread?"

"Certainly have—the Farnsworth place."

"I'm its new foreman," said Quinta. "Quinta, by name. The hungry one there is Zach Lankford. I hear you run the community bulletin board."

"For a fact I do."

Quinta took out a folded piece of paper and handed it to the barkeep, who unfolded it to read, "'Wanted . . . working hands . . . forty a month and found.' Nice wage, Mr. Quinta. If I was younger, I'd hire on."

A chair scraped, and Quinta looked over at another table to see a cowhand moving over. The stranger said, "Couldn't help overhearing what Joe here read from that paper. Mind if I join you a minute, Mr. Quinta?"

"Grab a chair," he said, liking what he saw of the cowhand. "Ah, barkeep, bring another shot glass and some cold beer for . . ."

"Jud Walker." He grasped Quinta's extended hand and shook it.

"Our cook, Zach Lankford."

"That's only temporary, Quinta. Just so's I can build up a grubstake."

"You keep treating like this, Zach, and that'll never happen."

"Mr. Quinta, four days ago I was gainfully employed by the Lazy M—Matt Candry's place up north of Greybull. Myself, and Pratt and Sundeen, those I was drinking with over there, were up mending fences, maybe two, three miles from the ranch site, when we heard gunfire. So we headed over there." In the hand's voice was a deep, controlled anger. "But too late to stop that damned T-Bar bunch from committing murder. To make a long story short, they'd brung the marshal from Greybull along, with the marshal claiming that Candry drew on Tex Whitney first. It's a bad thing when the law backs up out-and-out murder. Well, Mr. Quinta, then the marshal shows us a paper Matt Candry had supposedly signed deeding his ranch over to Charlton Talbot. There was maybe fifteen of those murdering swine. So after they cut out we set about burying Candry, found a couple of bullet holes—burn marks on his body where they'd used a hot branding iron on him. A man can't take too much of that before he caves in, I reckon."

"Talbot sure thinks he's top dog in the basin," Quinta said bitterly. "What are your plans now, Jud?"

"Finding work," said Walker, a solidly built man of medium height with a face seamed by years of ranch work and thinning sandy hair. "So are Pratt and Sundeen." He motioned the others over to Quinta's table.

Ed Pratt was a wiry, slat-faced man. The other hand, Marv Sundeen, had a blocky upper body tapering to a slim waist, a small scar slanting across his long nose and crinkled eyes. Both men wore Levi's, and leather vests

79

over work shirts and hats that had more than once been used as buckets to water their horses. They had the look of distance in their eyes, as did Jud Walker, an ease of movement that revealed itself when they settled down around the table.

"Would you men consider hiring on at the 77 spread?"

Walker looked at the others, and then he said, "That would suit us just fine, Mr. Quinta. It isn't the extra pay so much—but the need to get back at the T-Bar."

"Talbot's taking over the Lazy M means he controls both ways out of the basin," said Quinta.

"Doesn't public domain mean that everybody has a right to travel on or along the Big Horn River?"

"It shore does," spoke up Ed Pratt. "I know of some ranchers who were bringing their herds south along the river. Then here comes some of those damned T-Bar hired guns to charge toll fees. Other herds those hired guns stampeded."

"Why doesn't somebody send for the U.S. marshal?"

"I hear the marshal's too busy pocketing bribe money given him by Talbot."

"Now would be a good time to check out Granite Pass, Zach."

"Be pretty tough getting that supply wagon up there."

Quinta returned Lankford's smile and refilled his shot glass. "I figure you boys know a lot more about cattle than me or Lankford. Think we can get a herd up into them mountains?"

"Be safer using Powder River Pass," said Walker.

"Thought about that," replied Quinta. "But it comes out onto T-Bar land. Going up the other pass all we have to worry about is falling rock or an avalanche. Maybe one of you men can loan your horse to Zach."

Two days passed before Moses Quinta and the new men arrived at the 77 spread. Out of the ranch house came Celia and Sara, and over to where Quinta had stopped the supply wagon by the windmill. To Quinta's surprise he'd found that he had missed Celia, the kind of life he'd been leading here, and then he introduced those he'd hired to the Farnsworths, telling Celia also about what had happened up at the Lazy M Ranch.

"Glad to have you men here," Celia said around a smile. "This is Sara, my youngest. My other daughters are checking the herd over. Get squared away at the bunkhouse—we'll have supper in about an hour." When the others had left, she turned inquisitive eyes upon Quinta again to inquire as to the whereabouts of her cook.

"Sent Zach on an errand, ma'am."

"Quinta, damnit, you're up to something!"

"Simmer down, ma'am," he said soothingly.

"I see by your bloodshot eyes that you had a marvelous time in Worland," she said sarcastically.

"Opportunities like that don't come around too often. But I did manage to bring you back three able-bodied men."

"You should have brought back four. Now, where's Lankford?"

"Up checking out Granite Pass."

"Have you been chewing loco weed, Quinta? There's no way I'm going to take my cattle up in those Godforsaken mountains." She brushed a wind-blown lock of hair away from her glaring eyes.

Quinta jerked his hat lower over his forehead and uncoiled the reins from the hand brake lever. "There ain't no way Talbot is gonna let your herd pass onto his land without maybe you or one of your daughters getting hurt—or worse. Going up into them Big Horns just might be the only chance you've got of saving this place. Savvy!" Clucking at the horses, he brought them into motion and rolled away.

Zach Lankford let the roan set its own pace through the foothills. Mostly they were barren of trees, with an occasional outcrop of gray rock. Coming onto the lower reaches of the mountain, he heard the gurgling of fast-moving water before he came over a rise and upon brush and trees screening a creek. The land was climbing stiffly and Lankford rode at a walk until he came to a clearing, where he stopped to study the blocking pinnacles of rock shaped like the battlements of a monstrous castle. They seemed to form a barrier that would keep the plainsman from the upper reaches of the mountain. In moving on, he scared up an elk, the antlered animal pivoting with one great leap taking it through underbrush and out of view.

"Granite Pass is aptly named," mumbled Lankford, knowing that he would have preferred being astride his cayuse instead of this cutting horse, though it seemed sure-footed enough on the rougher, rock-laden ground they were traveling over.

He came to an abrupt break as if there were a door in the mountain, and went that way, with still more rocky spires to either side, taller than the first ones he'd encountered. The land opened up around him, narrowing some when he came to a track that would give him access to the heights he sought. Above Lankford, the pine forest of the mountain was thinner than he'd found in other sections of the Big Horn range.

Lankford's bronc climbed with a slow, choppy rhythm up the hard, bouldery ravine. On the few level places he dismounted to let the horse breathe, and either rode or walked to the next one. At a height the plainsman figured to be around five thousand feet, he rested again and gazed beyond his lowering back trail at the westward prairie opening up to him, and the snowcapped mountains beyond. Specks of movement were discerned by Lankford as pronghorns. With his index finger he reached into his mouth and scooped out the wad of snuff, took another pinch from his snuff box and placed it against his cheek before easing into the saddle. The roan swung sideways in its reluctance to climb any higher, sweat staining its shoulders and withers.

"Enough of that," muttered Lankford as he urged the bronc along the track, its shod hoofs sending loose pebbles trickling downhill.

When the plainsman reached a high plateau, its broad sweep of timber-littered land leveling into the deeper recesses of the mountain, he let the horse rest again. Walking down the track to where it plunged sharply, he studied its width, thinking that it was more a game trail than a place you'd bring up a large herd of cattle. There was the frightening chance that the leaders would swing around and pile into those coming behind. Far below in the bluish haze of the foothills a golden eagle appeared and flew about in tight circles until it caught an updraft, the eagle climbing now on rigid wings and in wider circles until it became a feathered speck above where Lankford stood. This was the trail of eagles, not for earthbound critters that had a tendency to break and run at the crackle of lightning or a tarp being torn loose by the wind and pounding against a chuck wagon. As a gambling man,

Zach Lankford knew this would be a high risk venture; some would die, and he didn't just mean cattle.

Moving back to the roan and mounting, he said, "Wagh, hoss, let's push on to the first water hole."

Under the ponderosas, the few stands of flickering aspens which permitted more sunlight to filter through, there was little underbrush, the grass sparse too but reaching above the fetlocks of his bronc. There was also dead timber, and Cloud Peak tucking its snowy head far above toward a cobalt-blue sky.

Lankford rode, by his reckoning, five miles before he came to a large meadow, and still there was mountain above him, but in the distance. Great heaps of rock were scattered about, sheer cliffs that rose to higher elevations. From his travels atop this range he knew about creeks and lakes and meadows such as this covered with alpine flowers and bear grass.

When the bronc caught the scent of water, it tossed its head, and then Lankford let it lope along at a pace which brought him to a marshy pond fed by a mountainous stream, where he set about making camp. He'd head back in the morning, seeing no need to scout any further, and wanting some of those rainbow and brown trout basking in the deep clear waters. For a few moments the plainsman was tempted not to go back, to summer up here for a spell, but the dictates of his conscience told him he'd hired out to a woman who needed help.

"Mrs. Farnsworth does for a fact," he murmured with some reluctance, though the temptation to remain here was still there as he inhaled deeply of mountain air, casting his eyes upon the jagged peaks again.

9

In every herd of wild range cattle, Jud Walker was telling Quinta, there were leaders willing to take on a marauding puma or grizzly or come onto the point, with one of them shoving ahead of the others and taking the herd where the cow boss wanted it to go.

"Take that old mossyhorn," Walker went on. "I figure it to have leadership qualities." The steer tossed its wide rack of horns as if it knew the horsemen were discussing its good points, with scars in the mottled brownish hide. A low bellow of defiance came from the mossyhorn as it ambled into a bunch of cattle to shoulder some aside in search of grass.

They'd been culling cattle out of underbrush growing on several humpbacked ridges separated by deep arroyos that were brush-littered and dead-ended or lifted back to the prairie. It was hard work, thorny brush tearing at them, dust boiling to blind or cause a steer to disappear again, the whiplash of oak or cottonwood branches almost tearing a rider out of the saddle. The days were cooling as autumn began to make its presence known, leaves beginning to turn and the sky going kind of steely-gray at times toward the horizon.

The days were growing short for Celia Farnsworth too, and she'd been ready to fire Zach Lankford after he'd come back to tell them cattle could be driven up Granite Pass. Celia still insisted upon taking the northern route out of the basin in spite of the fact that some of Talbot's hired guns would be waiting up there. Despite the ranchwoman's aloof attitude, Quinta sensed that she wanted to lean on a man for support, sort of wanting to reach out, but all that pride was holding her back. For someone calling this high country home, it was plumb irrational how Celia Farnsworth wouldn't listen to any talk of the Big Horns. Quinta had heard of those who were afraid of mountainous heights, but in Celia's case it could be a different reason.

"That Petrie kid is sure taking hold."

"Noticed that, Jud. The boss lady worries me—about her wanting to go across Lazy M land."

"I'd be worried too, Moses, if I took my daughters on a cattle drive. You asked me before what I thought about our chances up in them Big Horns. Handled right, I figure, it can be done. But that means every able-bodied man has got to work the cattle."

"When we start the drive, Jud, I want you to be cow boss. I'll ride drag so's I can watch out for Talbot's men."

"Appreciate your trust in me, Moses." Walker pulled out the makings and rolled a cigarette into shape.

"When Raoul Dixon gets back we'll get an idea just how many hired guns Talbot has on his payroll."

Striking a wooden match against his belt buckle, Walker lit his cigarette and inhaled deeply. "Just so Dixon can be trusted."

"In my trade, Jud, you learn right quick who to trust. Dixon will play it square now that he's setting his hat for

Celia's daughter." Then, at Quinta's nod, Walker swung his horse around, with those watching the cattle also tensing when three riders topped a rise to the north.

"It's Ben Tygee," said Quinta. Spurring that way, and with Jud Walker moving alongside, their broncs swerved around thorny brushes and up the red-clay bank of the arroyo to rolling land where they reined up.

"See you're still here, Quinta," said Tygee around a pleasant smile.

"Settling down to ranch life, I guess."

"Spotted your dust about a half hour ago. I'm on my way to see your boss, but me and the boys will lend a hand if you're heading that way."

"Appreciate it." Quinta waved his hat, and those watching the cattle brought them into motion, a shambling walk that carried the herd of around three hundred cattle in a ragged line up onto the prairie. The mossyhorn hung back from the leaders, perhaps sensing that it wouldn't be driven too far.

"Quinta, I got word to most of the ranchers," Ben Tygee said quietly. "The meeting's set for tomorrow afternoon down at Silver Springs."

"Did they sound interested?"

"Wary, mostly. But give them a good argument and they'll tag along."

Celia Farnsworth still wasn't certain if she'd done the right thing by hiring Raoul Dixon. Strange, also, she mused, that he'd shown up after her foreman and the other hands had ridden out to gather more cattle, but his argument to her had been of Raoul Dixon's disillusionment with the methods used by the cattle baron Charlton

Talbot, sending out his hired guns to harass the smaller ranchers, and of Dixon telling her how one of them, Tex Whitney, had gunned down the owner of the Lazy M Ranch. She hadn't put too much credence in what Dixon had told Quinta when they'd met down by the Big Horn River, since it was her firm opinion that anyone who'd work for Talbot must be like-minded. She would have sent Dixon packing had not Beth insisted that they hire him. The other young man, Petrie, Celia had discovered, was solid and dependable, would make someone a fine husband; Raoul Dixon had wanderlust in his dark eyes.

But the presence of Raoul Dixon caused a remarkable change in Beth Farnsworth. Her sunnier disposition affected the other girls, and this morning Celia had surprised herself by telling her cook to butcher a steer, that tonight when the hands returned there was to be a barbecue.

From the sanctuary of the house, and through a living room window, Celia could see the herd spread over several thousand acres of ranchland, the distant forms of her daughters keeping watch, and now, much to Celia's intense surprise, again came disturbing thoughts of Moses Quinta. Why!—spoke up Celia Farnsworth's conscience—he's a gunfighter, someone with blood on his hands, and it would take years to housebreak Quinta!

"Must be getting addle-brained," she murmured, crossing toward the kitchen where she found Zach Lankford, looking somewhat more tidy than when she'd first encountered him, sitting on a low stool by the open back door and peeling large red potatoes. Steam sputtered from kettles heating on the cast-iron stove, and on the table several pies were cooling, the aroma of baked apples coming to her.

"That beef's a-stewing in the barbecue pit, ma'am." He glanced over at her, then smiled. "My, but you sure got a sparkle in your eyes."

"I . . . have?" Celia found herself blushing. Then to her amazement she realized that touching secret parts of her body were feelings she'd suppressed ever since becoming a widow. This would never do, she scolded herself. "Seems you have everything under control."

"Yup, settling in to cooking."

"Zach," she said pensively, "I've heard getting up Granite Pass isn't all that easy."

"Nothing's easy, ma'am. But what I've seen of that pass, it can be done."

"I hate to think of going that way, especially with fall coming on."

"They're your cattle, ma'am. Tell me, is it true your daughters will make that drive?"

"I certainly wouldn't think of leaving them here, Zach. Why?"

"Was me, I'd think twice about bucking that rancher's hired guns. Cattle can be replaced—but not them daughters of yours, I'm reckoning."

"Well, Zach, think I'll ride out and check my herd over."

Lankford pointed with his paring knife at a basket resting on a counter by the sink. "Something I threw together for the girls—lemonade and some sandwiches."

"You shouldn't be catering to them, Zach."

"Well, ma'am, they sort of grow on a person." Then he unleashed a stream of tobacco juice out the back door.

Astride her favorite horse, a bay with a white star on its forehead and patches of white along its fetlocks, Celia rode out on the prairie, the wind barely stirring, the air somewhat cooler now that summer had about run its long course. She moved around bunches of cattle either grazing or lying down, and about a mile out, Celia pulled up under shade cast by a large cedar and waved her daughters in. Amanda and Sara arrived first, then Beth who'd been further out and on the northern fringes of the herd ground. Groundhitching their horses, the girls sat down to cluster around the picnic basket.

"Girls," scolded Celia, "you've got canteens to slake your thirst. And you'll only get consumption from eating between meals."

"Uncle Zach did this on his own, Ma," complained Sara as she reached for a sandwich. "Besides, I like lemonade."

"Uncle Zach? Now isn't that just peachy. What else has that plainsman been teaching you?"

"Things," said Amanda. "And he knows a lot of jokes too."

"Never thought my girls would sell out for a batch of lemonade," said Celia as she swung her horse around and rode away to hide her smile. Once the herd arrived at Sheridan, Zach Lankford would probably move on. She was growing fond of the plainsman, knew that underneath the rough exterior there was a gentle, wise man, so unlike her foreman. As Celia rode up onto an elevation, she saw Raoul Dixon riding toward her daughters. Remembering back to her courtship days, she knew that any unkind words from her about Dixon might see Beth pack up and leave the 77. Though she trusted her daughter's judgment, could it be that Beth's mind was clouded over by her love for Raoul Dixon? Then again, her husband, Buck, had always been one to give strangers a fair chance, at hiring on here or becoming friends.

Celia's thoughts were distracted by the distant rumble of thunder coming from a thunderhead trying to form off to the southwest and beyond Washakie Needles in the Shoshones. But the grayer tint near the horizon caused worry to film Celia's eyes—the color of winter, she knew. Conjuring up images of other days of late summer coming onto autumn, a summer blizzard could plunge out of the northwest and blanket the plains with snow. They had maybe two, two-and-a-half weeks left before the drive could start, and if they did head up Granite Pass, it would take at least a week to travel over those mountains, with almost a fifty-fifty chance of a storm catching them up there. It was such a storm that had trapped Buck's father on those heights, and after it was over, Celia had insisted upon going along to help search for him. Nearly four days later they'd found the body in a little valley under the prow of Mather Peak. Both of the horses he'd taken along had simply disappeared, leaving Buck's father propped up against the trunk of a ponderosa and staring at them out of sightless eyes. For a long time afterwards Celia suffered from the memory of what had happened, mostly blaming herself, because of her desire at that time to have the robe of an elk for her marriage bed.

Now a drifting cloud seemed to form the facial image of the gunfighter, Quinta, and she murmured, "Not again?" Her mind was turning contrary to its true nature. She'd know what love was, having been married to steady Buck Farnsworth those many years. These strange feelings she was having for Quinta had no source, as if they belonged to someone else, or came from untapped sources within her. Why, she knew her own mind as well as the ways of the basin: when it was going to snow, the time for calving. This mind change troubled Celia, but she was determined to rid herself of it before Moses Quinta returned to the ranch. What she needed to cleanse her thoughts was a swim in the creek, and with her mind set, Celia spurred back to her daughters.

Coming down a ridge and onto the herd ground, the riders let the cattle they'd brought in scatter into smaller bunches and fan out to mingle with those already grazing there. The sky was purling into dusk, and in the distance a coyote yapped as Sara Farnsworth galloped up on her piebald to exclaim, "We're going to have a barbecue!"

"My, but you've grown, Sara," said Ben Tygee. "Guess it won't be too long before some young man comes a-calling."

"Boys are dumb," she said. "And all Beth and Amanda do anymore is talk about their boyfriends."

As the little cavalcade went at a walk toward the buildings, Quinta asked Sara where he could find her mother, and offhandedly she informed him that Celia was down at the creek. "Better check in," said Quinta. "Jud, get these boys squared away at the bunkhouse."

Quinta rode behind the barn and past some haystacks, where he took a final drag on his cigar butt before flipping it down at hardpan. Then he moved under a cottonwood overlooking brush lining the creek, only to have his horse shy away as he caught a glimpse of white, with the bushes stirring in front of him and Celia Farnsworth hissing angrily, "Damnit, Quinta, you've got some nerve coming down here when I'm taking a swim. You—you peeping Tom!"

"Easy now, ma'am," Quinta explained. "Your daughter told me you was here."

"I'll bet!" snapped Celia. "Vamoose, Quinta!"

"I'll do that," he muttered. "Just wanted to tell you—" he wheeled his horse around—"that Ben Tygee and some of his men are here." And the gunfighter was still muttering to himself when he dismounted by a pole corral and unsaddled his horse. "That woman's skittish as a colt."

When Quinta entered the bunkhouse, a bottle was being passed around by Ben Tygee, who was in the midst of narrating a hunting story. After Tygee had finished telling his story, nobody started another one, and there wasn't the usual exchange of small talk either, for these men knew that dangerous times lay ahead. But Quinta could see that they weren't downcast; they looked like men who'd welcome anything the T-Bar could throw at them. Back at Silver Springs, Tygee had informed Quinta that five of the seven hands working out at his O Bar T spread would make the drive, the others staying behind to tend to chores. The men Tygee had brought along were getting along in years, and Quinta's silent appraisal was that both of them could handle themselves in a gunfight or around cattle. But they were only ten in number, not counting the Farnsworth women and Zach Lankford, and wanting some information about Talbot's hired guns, Quinta went over and propped a boot on the bunk that Raoul Dixon was sitting on.

"Well, Mr. Dixon, did you quit or did Talbot send you over here?"

"Señor Talbot still believes I am working for him."

"You've got spunk, that's for sure, Raoul. What I need to know is, how many hired guns does Talbot have on his payroll? And how many did he send up to the Lazy M?"

"There are about thirty in number, Señor Quinta. I

93

believe about ten of them were sent up to the Lazy M. The others, the working hands, live out at line shacks. I overheard Tex Whitney say that Señor Talbot has sent for a half dozen more hired guns."

"Whitney's out of Texas, if I recollect properly." It seemed strange to Quinta that the cattle baron would send Dixon over here as a spy. Without question, Talbot must know that Celia intended to make that drive to Sheridan. As for size, the 77, Celia had told him, was about the fourth largest ranch in the basin. Why was Charlton Talbot concentrating a lot of his attention on the 77? That the man wanted to buy Celia's ranch was no mystery, but Quinta had the notion it was more than that. He voiced these questions to Raoul Dixon, who responded with what he knew about the cattle baron, giving Quinta a better idea as to the plans of Talbot. Still, he needed another piece to complete the puzzle.

"I suppose, Raoul, the T-Bar will bring their herd out the southern route?"

"They intend to leave the ranch in a couple of weeks. But the hired guns will remain behind."

"Yeah," Quinta said bitterly, "to keep the other ranchers from getting their herds out."

As the dinner bell sounded, Quinta announced to the others that he'd stay behind and wash up before joining them for supper. Alone, the realization rode strong in him that Charlton Talbot was a changed man, one who didn't believe in putting all of his eggs in one basket. When they'd rode together, Talbot would tell Quinta of the dreams he had, with Quinta not expecting to be used as a stepping stone to fulfill them. And only when he came face to face with Charlton Talbot would Quinta be able to satisfy his curiosity just as to what the years and a

94

lot of prideful ambition had done to his old robbing partner. While Quinta had lived by the gun, the cattle baron had used the guns of others to get what he wanted, but mainly to do his killing. Maybe that was the way it was meant to be, but there was the agony of being backshot by Talbot along with the five years carved out of his life. That counted for something, maybe not in monetary gain, but in the knowledge that he was going to stand up to Talbot and settle this one way or another.

"Old partner, don't make no long-range plans," said Quinta as he filled the wash basin with fresh water and contemplated his stubbled face in the mirror. Before, he had it in mind to shave, and maybe douse himself with some lilac water he'd bought up in Worland, and now that stinging rebuke from Celia Farnsworth soured his mood, with thoughts of Talbot not helping either. Though he hated to admit it, the woman was getting to him, starting a softening process in him that could prove fatal if they encountered any T-Bar hands during the cattle drive. In the past, meanness had been his stock in trade, sort of like the Buntline Special worn by Wyatt Earp, or Wild Bill Hickok's big pancake hat. Where those he'd faced in a gunfight were worried more about what they'd tell the law afterwards or if their weapons would jam, Moses Quinta's one burning thought had been to simply kill the man he was facing. It was all reflex anyway, the draw, the Peacemaker seeming to point of its own accord at a vital spot for a split second before it bucked in Quinta's hand. The sudden rap at the door startled Quinta, and his hand strayed toward his holstered gun before he spat out, "It ain't locked."

The door creaked open to reveal Celia Farnsworth standing on the threshold and looking stunningly beautiful in a dark brown floor-length dress that had a high neckline and long sleeves. With some effort Quinta's eyes managed to life from about her waistline to Celia's face.

"I owe you an apology, Mr. Quinta," she said hesitantly.

"You mean about me coming upon you down at the creek?"

"Sara told me what happened. I guess—well, I did jump to conclusions."

"That happens, sometimes." Quinta reached for the shaving mug.

"You will accept my apology?"

"Nothing to apologize for, Mrs. Farnsworth."

Entering, Celia eased down on a bunk and said, "You were right about getting the other ranchers together, Quin—ah, I mean, Moses."

Quinta blinked away his surprise.

"Seeing as how we're getting to know one another a little better, let's try using our first names."

"You sure about that, Farnsworth?"

"It's worth a try," said Celia, rising. "I'll see you at supper."

When Celia had left, Quinta took his time about shaving as he reflected on her unexpected appearance and changed attitude. To his recollection, no she grizzly had ever sat down with a shorn lamb, which was just what had happened here. Maybe under those petticoats, he pondered, she'd been hiding her rifle. The ranchwoman was acting entirely out of character, and Quinta had had enough trouble plumbing the mind of the old Celia without having to worry about trying to figure out a new one. "Working for a woman can sure be unsettling," he remarked, the thought, after he'd cleaned up, that carried Moses Quinta toward a table set up near the barbecue pit, where one of the hands was strumming on a banjo.

Quinta stopped just short of light being thrown by some coal oil lanterns to stare at those seated around the table or standing. For the first time in years he felt at ease, as if what he'd been seeking for so long a time was here. But the harsh reality of it was that he was a gunfighter, a man hired to kill if the need came up, and to move on when his job was done. That was the long and short of it, and even now as his eyes sought out Celia Farnsworth helping Zach Lankford cut up some beef, the realization came strong in him that she was a woman beyond his reach, as untouchable as the traceries of moonlight beaming silvery through the spreading oak tree he was standing under.

10

First light had revealed snow flurries tumbling out of a gray sky. The heavy wind had a chilly feel to it, and it swirled around the riders heading away from the 77 ranch house, chimney smoke coming from it lining straight out to the southeast. The clouds came in low, and they didn't have the look of rain in them, but shifted rapidly and with no discernible shape so that you more sensed than glimpsed them changing. As the rim of the sun poked over the Big Horns, gleams of sunlight poured through chinks in the clouds and shone on the riders, bringing a smile to Moses Quinta's face from where he rode alongside Ben Tygee and Celia. The higher reaches of the Big Horns were obscured by clouds, though now and then a peak could be seen, and westward the gray sky seemed to be a part of the other mountain ranges, the Rockies and Absarokas. The air had the cold feel of winter to it, and even though Celia Farnsworth hadn't voiced any comments about the weather, the worry of her thoughts revealed itself in the way she'd survey the sky from time to time.

Last night, Quinta and Ben Tygee had discussed the need to send some men ahead to scout out Silver Springs, their shared fear being that the cattle baron could have gotten wind of the meeting.

"Talbot could have some men waiting in ambush," Tygee had said. Quinta replied, "That seems to be his style."

And so sometime after midnight Jud Walker and Tygee's hired hands had headed south, and it wasn't until midmorning that the two ranchers and Quinta rode into Silver Springs and left their horses at the livery stable. With Celia walking between them, they hurried down Main Street, which was deserted but for a man leaning into the wind as he made his way upstreet toward the Antler Bar. Several horses were standing at the tie rails in front of the Edgemont House, with the wind wuthering under the arcade running along its wide fieldstone facade.

Passing under the arcade, Tygee turned down the collar on his sheepskin and nodded at the horses. "By their brands I see Willard and Luger are here."

"So's Mike Barth," confirmed Celia as she pointed at a grulla bearing the Rocking J brand.

"I was hoping more would show."

"Well, it's a start," said Quinta as he held the door open. Then he followed the others through an alcove and into the hotel, where the men removed their sheepskins while Celia took off her fur-lined coat and loosened the scarf from around her neck.

Off to their left was an open space where some of the locals sat around square tables playing cards; beyond that, Olaf Vigness, the hotel's owner, hovered over a glass-topped counter, behind which a cabinet with pigeonholes in it was affixed to the wall between two windows looking out onto a side street. Further along the same wall were several high-backed booths, some of which were occupied, while opposite stools lined a long counter. To Celia's right a staircase carried up to the second floor, the doorway beyond that opening onto a spacious dining room inside of which the other ranchers had congregated around a long table.

Olaf Vigness was a tall, thin, big-boned man wearing half-moon glasses. The flesh of his face was pasty and drawn tight across the bones as of someone suffering from consumption. He had a pronounced Norwegian accent and a tight-lipped way of speaking. Clasped around his neck was a string tie, poking out of the breast pocket of his starched shirt were some pencils and the bowl of a pipe. When Vigness lifted his eyes from the ledger, the look he threw Celia and those with her was more grimace than smile.

"Velcome, Mrs. Farnsworth," he said. "Mr. Tygee."

"Seen any of Talbot's men around town?"

"Not for a couple of days, Mr. Tygee." Pulling out his handkerchief, he took a nervous swipe across his forehead. "Got orders from Marshal Ward that everyone must check their guns with me."

Anger flinting his face, Ben Tygee said, "You know better than to ask something like that, Olaf." Only Celia's presence kept the rancher from saying more, and those with him could see Tygee was struggling to keep his composure in the way he stiffened, the muscles growing tight along his jawbone.

Striding over to where he could see into the dining room, Quinta saw that the other ranchers were still carrying their weapons, and he turned to say, "The marshal knows where we'll be if he wants our weapons. Tell him too, Vigness, it's a damned disgrace him wearing that badge. Well, ma'am, ladies first."

101

"Thank you, Mr. Quinta," murmured Celia after she'd flicked the hotel owner a displeased glance. Removing her coat as she went into the dining room, she returned the smiles of the ranchers clustered around the table before draping her coat over others piled on a table, as Quinta and Tygee did with theirs.

"Celia, it was worth the trip to town just to see you."

"Why, thank you, Hank. How's Millie?" Celia found a chair at the table.

"Still got that back problem; other than that she's fine. Bring your daughters along?"

Celia said, "Somebody's got to mind the ranch."

As Tygee sat down to Celia's left, Quinta eased onto a chair at the end of the table, giving him a view of the front windows, the door he'd entered by and a service door opening onto the kitchen, through which came a waitress carrying a pot of coffee and a platter of hot rolls. During the exchange of small talk, Quinta sipped at the coffee while studying the ranchers, who were mostly middle-aged men and weathered, all of them wearing the harried looks of men who were experiencing hard times. He assumed that the hotel owner had asked the ranchers to check their guns, with all of them knowing that the order to do so had come from Charlton Talbot. At least, Quinta mused, we share a mutual distrust of the cattle baron.

"Boys, this is Celia's new *segundo*, Moses Quinta," piped up Tygee.

"My pleasure," said Quinta.

Rising, Ben Tygee stepped to the opposite end of the table to make the introductions. Hank Willard was a bulky man with pleasant features; Bill Kiley had a handlebar mustache below a crooked nose, and he kept drumming his stubby fingers on the table; Mike Barth and Harley Luger were large men, and where Barth was balding, Luger had thick black hair with an ashy streak running back from his left temple; the last one, Charley Moore, regarded Quinta through cynical blue eyes, letting the gunfighter know that he didn't care too much for that line of work, and wasn't too pleased about being asked to attend this meeting by Ben Tygee.

Kiley stopped drumming his fingers long enough to say, "It's damned unlawful Talbot charging us toll fees for bringing our cattle across his land. Now that he's more or less stolen the Lazy M, we could be up the creek."

"Unlawful or not, we're all facing the same problem. Mostly though, we can't go alone against all of Talbot's hired guns. The only solution is to pool our herds."

"Ben, we take that many cattle to Sheridan, it'll drive the market price way down."

"That's hogwash, Charley, and you know it," countered Tygee.

"I always managed to get my herd to market," spoke up Harley Luger. "And no damned renegade cattle baron is gonna stop me now. I agree with Charley, that we should go it alone."

"Do that," Quinta said, "and you'll be playing Talbot's game. I'm backing up Mrs. Farnsworth's suspicions that some of Talbot's hired guns killed her husband. And for a fact, Tex Whitney backshot the owner of the Lazy M."

Charley Moore shoved his cup away and he said skeptically, "I heard the marshal of Greybull was there when it happened. According to him, Matt Candry went for his gun first."

Quinta's lips formed a tight line around the cigar, and

he said softly, "You can't legalize murder. Nobody forced any of you to come to this meeting. But I figure your choice is clear-cut—pool your herds or take your chances alone."

In the uneasy silence following what Quinta had said, the ranchers seemed to withdraw within themselves as they pondered over what they were going to do next. Suddenly there came the clumping of boots as one of Tygee's men appeared to stand framed in the doorway. "A bunch of riders is coming in!"

"Talbot's men?"

"Appears to be."

"Somehow Talbot found out about the meeting?" Tygee said questioningly as he gazed at each rancher in turn, the eyes of the others holding steady with his until Tygee came to Charley Moore, who reddened some as he looked away. Exhaling wearily, he asked, "Why, Charley?"

Under the scrutinizing gaze of Tygee and the others, Charley Moore's face clouded with anger. He rapped the knuckles of his clenched fist down at the table a couple of times—a nervous gesture, thought Quinta—before framing a defiant scowl. "Talbot came to my place," he said sullenly. "Wanted to buy me out. I told him I'd let him know."

"You also told him about the meeting," Celia said accusingly.

"More or less." Charley Moore shoved away from the table to rise from the chair. "But not before Talbot told me about his men stringing barbed wire down along the flood plain and clear east to the Big Horns. Hell, he owns most of the basin anyway."

"How about up north, Charley?" questioned Hank Willard.

"Up there, too. Damnit, he's got us boxed in. Selling out to Talbot is the only chance I've got left." Moving over, he retrieved his sheepskin. "Stay if you want. Pool your cattle; whatever you do, I figure Talbot's got the upper hand." Settling his hat over his head, Charley Moore hurried out of the dining room.

The other ranchers felt the sting of what Charley Moore said, and they sat silently for a few moments, trying to decide whether to oppose Talbot or sell out and slink out of the basin. By coming here, all of them knew that they'd already taken a stand against the cattle baron, but now, in the final minutes left to them before Talbot and his hired guns reached Silver Springs, there was indecision, a survivor's instinct taking hold. Mike Barth, who up until now had been content to listen to the others, rose to tell his fellow ranchers that he'd decided to try to make a deal with Talbot, and he left.

"For a fact," said Hank Willard, "Mike is more worried about his five yonkers than about what's happening here. Ben, Celia, I've got around seven hundred head of prime beef ready for market. And I'd consider it an honor if I could throw my herd in with yours."

Bill Kiley rose and hitched at his gun belt, and he laughed nervously before saying, "Them's my sentiments. Most of you have got more to lose than I have. What I'm saying is, folks, I can't ask for better neighbors than what I've got."

"Well," said Ben Tygee, "let's go see what that cattle baron wants."

Out under the arcade, the wind shrilling around the ranchers didn't have the snapping bite to it of this morning while the cloud cover was beginning to break up. Quinta stood behind the others as he checked to see if

Jud Walker and Tygee's hired hands had spotted the incoming riders. Then Quinta caught a glimpse of Walker crouched on the roof of the Ranchester Saloon; one of Tygee's men was hiding in an alley, the other man out of sight but Quinta knew he'd be ready too. These men would only respond to any gunplay coming from Talbot's hired guns. Those standing under the arcade swiveled their heads downstreet when Marshal Ike Ward waddled out of the Ranchester Saloon and headed toward the Edgemont House, only to pull up short when he saw the waiting ranchers and, off to the southeast, the plume of dust kicked up by the horsemen heading toward Silver Springs. Making an abrupt about-face, the marshal scurried back into the saloon.

"So much for law and order," Celia said scornfully.

"Maybe you should wait inside?"

"Damnit, Hank, I'd like nothing better than to part Talbot's hair with a slug from my Smith & Wesson."

There was a moment of blindness when a burst of sunlight came through a rift in the clouds, and then the horsemen were clattering onto the stagecoach road and heading toward where it crossed over the narrow-gauge tracks. There was no mistaking Carlton Talbot, dressed fancier than those riding with him, astride a rangy black thoroughbred and with sunlight glinting off of golden ornaments adorning the heavy saddle, but the rancher rode well back in the pack of riders and not out front as their leader, that position taken by his *segundo*, Tex Whitney.

Somehow Moses Quinta was struck with the notion that the hired guns were more Talbot's bodyguards than anything else. Now Quinta tried to dislodge from the darkness of his memory the Talbot he'd known before.

106

Though some memory chords were struck, the Charlton Talbot coming onto Main Street with the others bore little resemblance to the one Quinta had known. I've changed too, mused Quinta, lost the peach fuzz and innocence of youth a long time ago, but the bitterness of what Talbot had done to him, when they were robbing together and of late down at Cheyenne, brought an angry glint to Quinta's eyes.

Then the T-Bar hands were fanning out to come at a lope along Main Street, the stamp of outlaw upon them, men to whom killing was a daily chore, and who'd grown to like watching others suffer. Quinta always felt he was different than these men, but the fact remained that he'd hired his guns to Celia, and if it was his turn to die today, well, that was the roll of the dice. Now he stepped between Celia and Ben Tygee.

The cattle baron tugged back on the reins when he saw Quinta. His horse cantered sideways but Talbot never took his eyes off the gunfighter. Then the hired guns were riding past to form a half-circle in the street before the Edgemont House, the harsh fact that they outnumbered the ranchers causing smug smiles to appear as they glanced sideways at one another.

Charlton Talbot wore an imported English hunting coat, and instead of a Stetson, a sable cap, but under the coat he had on a tailored cattleman's suit and spurred cowboy boots. Thrust into the saddle boot along with the Winchester was a gold-headed cane. Coldly, almost indifferently, he surveyed those he'd come to see, and finally, he put words to his thoughts.

"It's been a long time, Moses."

"Not long enough," came Quinta's taut reply.

"I hear you're working for the 77 spread."

"That about sums it up. You seem to have made a success of things, old partner." By Quinta's count there were seventeen hired guns, but would Talbot try anything with Celia here, or even here in Silver Springs where there were townspeople peeking out of windows and doors?

Now the cattle baron turned his attention to the other ranchers, saying smoothly, "In the past my offers to buy your property have been spurned. You, Mrs. Farnsworth, are having a hard time of it, I've heard."

"Not any harder than my friends, here," Celia said quickly, her face darkening angrily under the impact of the cattle baron's penetrating gaze.

Like lamplight coming on to cast shadows out of a dark room, the mystery of why Charlton Talbot had come here today exploded in Moses Quinta's mind. Now he knew why Talbot was taking a special interest in the 77 Ranch, and why he'd sent Raoul Dixon as his spy. The simple truth of the matter was that the cattle baron was in love with Celia Farnsworth. The thought sickened Quinta, brought up a surge of jealousy and also made him realize why Talbot was making it so difficult for Celia and the othe ranchers to get their cattle to market. The ranch, in a way, was Celia Farnsworth, the sum total of all that she stood for, the source of her strength and love. By wresting the 77 spread away from Celia the cattle baron could break the woman's spirit, corral her, put his brand on her, bed Celia. Squinting against the sunlight, Quinta could see deep into Charlton Talbot's blue eyes and read there the feelings the man had for Celia, feelings that blinded the cattle baron to everything but his need to possess her.

Here he was, thought Quinta, Charlton Talbot, a man

consumed by greed, lusting for a woman who'd sooner blow his brains out than have anything to do with him, and he seemed to be even blinded to that. Nevertheless a man who'd let himself go physically and looked it, with that fleshy face and overweight frame encased in clothes only the rich could afford, but in his present condition, both of mind and body, a man more dangerous than a wounded grizzly, and as unpredictable. By stringing that barbed wire, Talbot had cut himself off from the other ranchers, and Quinta had the feeling that Talbot didn't give a damn either. Killing didn't seem to bother the cattle baron, but would there be bloodletting today? Perhaps not, because Quinta sensed that this was Talbot's final warning to other landowners or those opposing his killing methods. As the Holy Book said, the battle of Armageddon wouldn't take place here, reserving that, if Quinta remembered correctly, for the Plain of Megiddo, which out here in the basin could mean the southern route if some of the ranchers opposed to pooling their cattle tried to drive their herds that way. It wouldn't be too much longer, either, before Talbot turned loose his pack of killer dogs, so despite Celia's objections, they would have to go up Granite Pass in the Big Horns.

In his youthful days, Quinta's parents had often voiced their concerns about his reckless ways, and at the moment he could feel that old recklessness surfacing as he swung his eyes to a big man mounted on a gray, Tex Whitney. And by their own accord it seemed that Whitney's eyes came to rest upon Moses Quinta, who stepped out from under the arcade and further into the street to stop and spread his legs wide in a poise of grim defiance while flicking a glance at the cattle baron.

"I hear your *segundo* is pretty good at shooting unarmed men in the back."

"Say your piece," spat out Charlton Talbot.

"I figure Matt Candry wasn't heeled when he was killed. That Whitney backshot him. Who used that branding iron on Candry? You, Mason? Or you, Adair? Thought you got yourself hung down in Las Verdes. Or was it you, Whitney?"

"Quinta," sneered Tex Whitney, "you're talking loco! The marshal of Greybull said it was self-defense." He laughed jeeringly, with most of the others joining in.

"I'm happy to see you brought along all of your court jesters, Talbot," said Quinta. "Reckon there ain't a man with guts in the whole bunch."

"You picked a good day to die, Quinta!" snarled Tex Whitney as he swung a leg over the withers of his horse.

"Enough of this!" shouted Charlton Talbot. "Whitney, I told you there'd be no gunplay in Silver Springs. Disobey my orders and you're fired." He waited until Whitney had settled back in the saddle, then he said, "As for you ranchers, I haven't much patience left. I've offered all of you fair prices for your land."

"What about that wire you strung along the flood plain?"

"It's to keep my cattle from drifting, Mrs. Farnsworth."

"And if we try to get our cattle through?"

"A price has to be paid!" Casting a final look at the ranchwoman, Charlton Talbot swung his horse around and headed it toward the Ranchester Saloon, his hired guns riding to either side.

Turning to Quinta, Celia said, "You live dangerously, Moses."

"What you hired my guns for."

"Not to commit suicide, I didn't."

"Well, Harley," said Ben Tygee, "you can change your mind about not pooling your cattle."

"Mind's made up," Harley Luger said quietly. "But good luck to you folks." Swinging aboard his horse, he rode away.

"That leaves four of us," said Celia. "Let's go back into the dining room and talk this over." When they were seated around the table, much to Quinta's surprise, Celia suggested they head their combined herds up Granite Pass.

"Guess we'll have to now that Talbot's strung all that damned wire," said Hank Willard. "But it'll be risky."

"Maybe," said Quinta, "but with any luck we'll be out of the basin before Talbot finds out we've pooled our herds."

"Here's the way we can work it," said Ben Tygee as he took out a stub of pencil and began etching an outline of the Big Horn basin on the tablecloth

11

Harley Luger's H-Bar-L Ranch took up around five sections of land where the Greybull converged with the Big Horn River. For Luger and the other ranchers in the basin, the kind of weather they'd been having for the past week—mostly clouds with a few light snowfalls—indicated there would be an early winter, and if they didn't start their herds to market before too much longer, the passes could be blocked or they'd be snowbound along the way.

By moonlight Harley Luger could see the gleaming waters of the Big Horn from where he rode, most of the cattle he owned throwing up dust as his men headed them along the reaches of prairie touching onto the flood plain. On reflection, Luger knew that he should have pooled his herd, but his way of making do without asking others for help was a hard habit to break. His neighbors said that Harley Luger was too stubborn for his own good, and he would have to agree that they were right, though in his way of thinking Luger had nailed down his character traits to a strict Quaker upbringing before he'd broken free and made his way west some twenty years ago. He still had old-fashioned ideas about how things should be done, which to Luger meant forthright honesty and a man's word being his bond.

At the moment Luger's thoughts were fixed somberly on the barbed wire fence the cattle baron had put across his land and extending across the flood plain to seal off both banks of the Big Horn. The northern reaches of the cattle baron's land abutted Luger's, and ever since he'd returned from Silver Springs, Harley Luger had been having one of his men keeping a nightly watch on the fence. After nightfall, he'd found out, Talbot's men kept pretty much to the line shack some four miles west of the river.

Kneeing his horse into a lope, Luger rode along the flank of the herd until he encountered one of the point riders, and together they went past the leaders and to a spur of land overlooking T-Bar land.

"Who did you send ahead to cut the wire?"

"Jake and the Tisdale kid."

Worriedly Luger tried to pierce the mottled darkness, the footfall of the herd edging up from behind, the feeling that there would be trouble giving him second thoughts about going ahead with this. If they cleared the fence without incident, there was still some fifteen some miles of T-Bar land they'd have to cross before reaching the southern pass. Waiting until morning meant that he'd have to pay the toll fee of two bits a head the cattle baron was charging, and then Luger firmed up his decision to keep going when those riders who'd been sent ahead to cut the wire appeared.

"Boss, the way is clear. Just head toward that clump of trees."

"See any sign of Talbot's men?"

"Tisdale scouted over by that line shack; them hired

114

guns are bedded down for the night."

"Well, it's around eleven," said the rancher as he consulted his pocket watch. "Sunup should see us clearing the pass. Alright, men, let's do it!"

Luger and his men swung back to the herd. They brought the cattle at a walk down the long grade of prairie to where it levelled off as the gaping holes between the fence posts came into view, and once the leaders were through, the rest of the herd followed them southward. Though the herd wanted to spread out and rest or graze, Luger's H-Bar-L hands kept them on the move. The moon rose higher to send down liquid silvery light and agonizingly closer came the uneven chalkline of the Owl Creeks, with the herd coming onto the foothills now as they moved about a mile to the west of the cliff separating the prairie from the flood plain. And in the gray dawn chill coming onto the basin Harley Luger felt a sudden release of tension when his groping eyes spotted the pass opening up between the mountain ranges ahead.

"Another hour and we're out of this," he said around a tight-lipped smile.

From somewhere off to their right and further out on the prairie a horse whickered, and the hired hand Luger had spoken to threw a quizzical glance in that direction, but in the blackness still clinging to the land all he could see were the silent crowns of aspens littering a slope. Tugging at his hat, he said, "Probably a wild mustang."

"Could —" The deadly rattle of gunfire tore the rest of what Harley Luger was going to say out of his throat suddenly spouting crimson, and the rancher felt himself slipping out of the saddle. As a slug tore into the chest of the man Luger had been riding with, horsemen broke out of the tree line and came at the herd already breaking to head blindly to the east, the men on that side swept up into the maelstrom of stampeding cattle, those opposite returning the murderous fire of Talbot's hired guns before they were spilled out of their saddles.

Over the frightened lowing of the cattle, the drumming of thousands of hoofs striking the hard ground, came the terrified scream of a cowhand, which was abruptly cut off. Behind the herd the hired guns fired into and over the packed mass of cattle, then the leaders were plunging over the cliff, and even though some of those coming behind realized what was happening, the main body of the herd kept plowing frenziedly onward until only a few dozen head ran aimlessly away from the cliff edge.

The urge to kill was still a hot flame in Tex Whitney's thoughts as he wheeled his horse around and rode with the others in search of any survivors. Cattle had been trampled in the onrush toward the cliff, and their battered carcasses littered the prairie, along with those horses that had paid the price for being on the river side of the herd. There were also the mangled remains of cowhands recognizable only by tattered bits of clothing still clinging to flesh—and four in number by Turk Oldham's count. The bodies of the other hands lay where they'd fallen. Whitney and his men began checking for signs of life.

One of those still clinging to the spark of life was Harley Luger, and dimly he became aware of a pair of boots wearing roweled spurs jangling toward him, of a noise like dried walnut husks crackling underfoot as a gun was cocked. In the time left to him, the rancher tried desperately to focus upon deadly eyes glittering into his before Turk Oldham triggered his Navy Colt. The rancher's body jerked and quivered a few seconds and

116

then stiffened into death. Nearby, there was another muzzle flash, the reverberating report of the Henry barely dying away before a screech owl cut loose in the trees.

"Bury these men," Tex Whitney said coldly.

"Why not just toss them over the cliff?"

"Do it, or we'll plant you too." Whitney glared at the hired gun who'd spoken before wheeling his horse around in the general direction of the cliff. He rode away without a backward glance.

After fording the Big Horn, Tex Whitney cleared the flood basin to arrive at the main buildings just as Raoul Dixon came out of the ranch house and climbed aboard his bronc to ride away. He didn't have much use for Dixon, and earlier this summer he'd tried to goad the kid into a fight, but nothing had come of it.

"Dixon's a damned coward," he muttered as Charlton Talbot appeared in the patio. Leaving his horse at the tie rail, Whitney struck a match on his thumbnail and relit the cigarette dangling from his lips as he walked into the patio. "We didn't leave any witnesses."

"Good work." The rancher beamed. "But I want Marshal Ward to take a look at what they did to my fence before it's repaired. I should be able to buy Luger's ranch real cheap when it's auctioned off."

"You look pretty chipper this morning," commented Whitney.

"Celia—Mrs. Farnsworth—wants to meet me at Silver Springs."

"About selling out?"

Nodding, Talbot said, "I'm to see her day after tomorrow."

"Just doesn't sound right to me." But Tex Whitney's

statement fell on deaf ears as Talbot, a sort of lustful gleam in his eyes, turned on his heel and entered the house.

A few miles to the southeast, on the vast reaches of T-Bar land, Raoul Dixon draped his hands over the pommel of his standing horse while trying to figure out the size of the herd on the grasslands below him. They were mostly longhorns and white faces, clustered in large bunches of three or four hundred. They weren't grazing free but were being watched by most of the ranch's working hands. Spurring ahead, he rode toward the bundle and chuck wagons and some of the hands hunkered around a campfire.

"Got to be at least five thousand head," was Dixon's estimate. Grazing nearby was the remuda of some forty horses which the hands would use as they drove the cattle to the railhead at Sheridan.

Climbing down from his horse by the chuck wagon, Dixon received a friendly nod from the *segundo*, Bill Liscomb, who sat rocking on his haunches across the campfire as did the other hands. The cook tossed Dixon a tin cup and he filled it from the blackened pot hanging over the flames before he eased down.

"How's tricks, Raoul?" asked Liscomb.

"Getting by," was his response. "When you figuring on leaving?"

"Dawn tomorrow. You back to stay?"

"Hired me on at the 77 spread."

"Mighty convenient for you," said one of the hands, "since you're so sweet on that Farnsworth girl."

Dixon laughed with the others. Though he was glad to see Liscomb and others he'd ridden with, his real purpose for coming here revealed itself when he began the telling of how Celia Farnsworth intended taking her herd over Powder River Pass in the Big Horns. "Only thing she can do now that Talbot's got both ends of the basin fenced off."

"Some of Talbot's hired guns are watching Powder River Pass too," said Pat Zachery, the hard eyes in his blade-thin face going to Dixon. "No matter which way she takes her herd she's got to pay a toll fee."

"I hear there's another way over those mountains."

"There is," Zachery said derisively, "if you happened to be a mountain goat. You just don't take cattle up Granite Pass."

"Guess the 77 herd is boxed in," commented Dixon as he sipped at the thick black coffee.

"When is that ranchwoman figuring on leaving?"

Dixon looked at Zachery a moment before saying, "Probably be about a week before everything's squared away."

"Then take my advice," said Zachery.

"That being?"

"Tell your boss lady to pay that toll fee."

Coming erect, Raoul Dixon drained his cup and tossed it back to the cook, and voicing his goodbyes, he swung into the saddle and veered toward the north. Word of what he'd said, Dixon knew, would be carried back to the cattle baron. As he rode, Dixon let his mind fill with the image of Beth Farnsworth. During the time he'd been working at the 77, his feelings for her had intensified, made him pause occasionally to dream dreams of what life would be like with her as his wife. The only obstacle to his dream was Celia Farnsworth, who seemed to have taken an instant dislike to him. Would Beth marry him without her mother's blessings? Even now, pondered

Dixon, the ranchwoman was probably thinking that he wouldn't return.

And the gunfighter, Quinta, was just as hard a person to figure out, though he'd been making inroads into winning Quinta's trust.

Another factor that had come into play, and which caused an amused smile to tug at Raoul Dixon's mouth, was the way Moses Quinta got stiff-necked and on edge whenever him and the ranchwoman encountered one another, almost as if they were about to square off in a bare-knuckle brawl. There they were, Quinta, trying to mask what he truly felt about Celia Farnsworth, and her doing likewise. Dixon had the notion that they were falling in love. After all, Raoul Dixon was suffering the pangs of it, and it would serve the gunfighter right if he got corralled and branded.

"Quinta, you can't draw that Peacemaker and gun your way out of this one," Dixon said through a sudden burst of exuberant laughter, and then he spurred his bronc into a gallop, the dream he'd been dreaming lately bringing glimpses of the woman he loved brushing the roof of his mind.

12

The last tally taken by Celia Farnsworth's hands came to around eleven hundred head, but there seemed to be more cattle than that strung out as the herd was in the line of march. They wouldn't be touching civilization until they arrived at Sheridan, the plan laid out by Moses Quinta to avoid the towns of Worland and Greybull by bringing the herd along the foothills of the Big Horns.

Out here the law was measured in calibers, a fact which Quinta had tried to impress upon Celia because of her adamant insistence that her daughters go along. Walking may be the natural gait of cattle, he'd told her, with the herd covering about twenty miles in a day's travel, but once the cattle baron got tired of waiting for Celia to show up at Silver Springs, Talbot would put aces and eights together and send his hired guns after her 77 branded cattle, and they'd be coming hard.

These were the thoughts troubling Quinta as his sorrel labored up to a rocky promontory. Dragging cigar smoke into his lungs, he studied through the field glasses the Big Horn River shimmering in the far distance. Beyond the flood plain and to the northwest dust choking the horizon indicated the location of the herds the other ranchers had already mingled together. Once they brought their cattle across the river, they would make a beeline for the rendezvous point just north of Ogalla Creek. Another day and a half should bring them to the lower reaches of Granite Pass. From Raoul Dixon he'd found out that the cattle baron had taken on ten more hired guns, swelling their number to about forty. Opposing these killers would be nineteen men including Quinta and the Farnsworth women. Complicating matters would be the fact that Quinta's force would be burdened down with the cattle. And into the gunfighter's mind came the threads of last night's conversation with Celia.

"You look worried."

Celia Farnsworth turned her eyes away from the Big Horns shimmering under moonlight. "I'm still not sure that we're doing the right thing."

"There are times when a person has to make a hard decision."

"I know that, Moses, but—but taking my cattle up into those mountains . . ."

"Worrying won't help matters, Celia. I'd be thinking more about leaving your girls behind."

"Not as long as Talbot's murderers are on the loose. And I doubt if Dixon will be coming back."

"He'll be here. And come the dawning, Mrs. Farnsworth, things will look better."

"Tell me, Mr. Quinta, have you ever been married?"

At the time the question had caught Moses Quinta by surprise, and reflecting on it now as he put the field glasses back in the saddlebag, there had been a brief moment when they'd shared a certain closeness. Though he'd been tempted to take Celia into his arms, he'd let the moment pass, the clouds of what he was surfacing. Them getting together would be like trying to mix oil and water, and Quinta figured too, it would sure cramp his roaming style.

It had warmed up considerable, and though the prairie had little snow cover, patches of snow piebalded the foothills, while the Big Horns seemed taller than they really were, a few wispy clouds hanging under the peaks but the sky a sort of gun-metal blue and the moon hanging like a day star over the Absarokas. It felt good to begin the drive on this kind of day, the warmer weather serving to ease some of Quinta's worry.

Drawing on the cigar, he tracked southward, the passing of his sorrel scaring up a spike buck, which took a few prancing steps toward the mouth of an arroyo while its big brown eyes tried to plumb the horseman's intentions.

"Could use some venison," murmured Quinta as he eased his right hand down toward the scabbard and pulled out the Winchester, the clacking noise it made as he levered a shell into the chamber bringing the buck into motion. Quickly he sighted the rifle and fired, the heavy slug striking the deer in midstride and snapping its backbone. As the buck crumbled into some bushes, a smiling Quinta rode toward it.

Quinta was quartering the deer with his hunting knife when the clatter of hoofs jerked his eyes to the arroyo mouth and Celia Farnsworth's face set in angry lines. "Dammit, Quinta, that shot you fired could have stampeded the cattle!" By her side were Jud Walker, who had taken out his revolver, and Ed Pratt just drawing rein to his bronc.

"Well, I didn't, did I?" he snapped back.

"Quinta, I just don't know about you," said Celia as she shook her head.

"Ma'am," Quinta said as he went back to cutting at the carcass, "you've got no spirit of adventure."

"Right about now venison has a certain appeal to it," said Jud Walker, his smile for Celia easing some of her anger.

"It would be a change," she agreed. "I'll send Lankford over here with his pack horses. Any sign of the others?"

"They should bring the other herd across the Big Horn sometime this afternoon."

But it wasn't until dusk was settling on the prairie that the other herd reached a tract of land north of Ogalla Creek which was already being occupied by Celia's cattle. The herds came together to spread out more, and after milling about for a while, the cattle got back to the business of grazing. Except for the regular night horses and Zach Lankford's string of pack horses penned in a rope corral secured to trees, the mounts were grazing with the cattle. The fire Lankford had started was in the lee of a low bluff, the flames from it sending out waves of butter-colored light. The smell of frying venison kept most of the hands close to the fire where they were resting while waiting for the call to supper. And every two hours there would be a change of watch as some of those here would ride out to relieve the nightriders.

"I owe you an apology, Moses."

"That so?"

"It's been a spell since I've had venison."

Celia, Quinta and the other ranchers were clustered in

a little group by themselves as they talked over tomorrow's route and how they would handle the herd when they reached Granite Pass. They'd been told by Celia about how she'd sent Raoul Dixon down to Talbot's T-Bar spread.

"I see no reason why Talbot won't believe Dixon," said Ben Tygee as he balanced a cup of coffee on one knee where he sat with his back propped against his saddle.

"It should buy us a couple of days," said Quinta.

"Those new rifles you passed out are something," Hank Willard said.

"Beats using those old single shots," agreed Bill Kiley. "Just hope we don't have to use them."

"I'm hoping that the cattle don't get it in mind to stampede," said Celia, casting a sly glance Quinta's way. "Collecting a herd this size would take a lot of time."

"For certain I won't be taking any more pot shots at deer," Quinta said. He returned Celia's smile.

When the call for supper came, the men waited patiently until the women had filled their plates, then they formed a silent line, the worry of what lay ahead showing plain on their weathered faces. Some of them came back for a second helping, and when they were through eating, they dropped their utensils in the wash pot and headed for their bedrolls. The other cook brought along by Ben Tygee helped Zach Lankford tidy up the camp, and as Lankford sat down to take a break, which meant reaching for his harmonica, Celia made her way over to where Moses Quinta stood leaning against a tree overlooking the creek.

Glancing at her, he said, "Been thinking that two bucks a head is a stiff price for getting your cattle to market."

"I appreciate your concern about my finances, Quinta, but we made a deal which I intend to honor."

"You sure get your hackles up in a hurry, Mrs. Farnsworth."

Celia laughed softly. "The way I am." Her eyes went up to his face, and before Celia realized it she'd moved into his arms. Their lips came together, held for a brief moment, then abruptly both of them pulled apart to lock glances in silent wonderment.

"I had no intention of doing that."

Celia murmured, "Neither had I."

Quinta frowned and then swung around and left her standing there, the walk which carried him to where he'd spread out his bedroll under a tree accompanied by the realization that he had some soul-searching to do, along with the worry of what tomorrow would bring.

Settling into his blankets, and with his head up on his saddle, Quinta lit a cigar and puffed away at it while fixing his eyes on a sky blazing with stars. Celia could have sent that letter to any number of others who hired out their guns—Doc Holiday, Wild Bill Hickok, maybe even Ben Thompson. Then he'd still be loafing around Dodge City with just himself and his conscience to worry about. Somehow the thought of settling into married life brought a chill to his body. For certain he'd have a readymade family, but to frame words to say to Celia weren't, Quinta figured, natural to him.

"Nope, it just don't set right me thinking about getting hitched."

"You say something, Quinta?"

His face reddening, Quinta muttered to the hand who'd spoken, "Just dreaming out loud is all."

And Moses Quinta decided that come tomorrow he'd

126

go back to his old way of speaking harshly to the ranchwoman, which would serve to put them back on the more familiar and safer ground of disliking one another. Puffing away on his cigar, the gunfighter turned his mind to the more pleasurable way he would decorate the gambling casino he would build in Jackson Hole country.

13

The daylong presence in Silver Springs of Charlton Talbot and his hired guns kept most of the townspeople at home or places where they worked. Around midafternoon the stagecoach rattled onto Main Street and pulled up before the arcade in front of the Edgemont House. Some of the hired guns came outside, but lost interest when it didn't disgorge any passengers, so to amuse themselves they went back inside and started a poker game at one of the tables in front of the counter. But they didn't say too much because of the cattle baron's presence in the dining room.

Just before dusk the cattle baron summoned the owner of the hotel into the dining room and made inquiries as to whether or not Celia Farnsworth had told of her intentions to rent a room.

"I have not been informed of this," stammered Vigness.

Charlton Talbot wasn't a man who liked to be kept waiting, especially by a woman, and he made no attempt to hide his displeasure, or to be civil to the hotel owner. Upon arriving in town this morning, Talbot's first stop had been here at the hotel to tell Vigness that he was reserving the dining room for this evening. Then he'd left for the Ranchester Saloon to play some monte.

Dismissing the hotel owner with a wave of his hand, Talbot refilled the long-stemmed glass. With each tick-tock of the grandfather clock wedged in the southwest corner of the dining room chunks of the cattle baron's patience were breaking away. Though he'd taken special pains with his attire of a deep blue velour coat over a black vest with mother-of-pearl buttons, and black trousers with a crease so sharp in them that they could be used to cut butter, Talbot's face was pouched in that ugly look men get when a woman has stood them up. Ranch work could have delayed her, he pondered, or, as he suspected, he'd been suckered, that the 77 spread was moving their herd to market.

Yesterday, word had been brought to him of Celia Farnsworth's intentions to take her herd over Powder River Pass. He hadn't put much credence in the idea simply because he didn't fully trust Raoul Nixon. Smothering his anger, he pondered over the route that the 77 would take as he shouted Tex Whitney into the room.

"You were right about Dixon. I want him gunned down. If the 77 spread has their cattle on the move, so do the other ranchers."

"Meaning those who wanted to pool their herds?"

"Yes, damnit! They certainly won't risk taking the southern route out of the basin."

"Zachery said there was talk of using Granite Pass."

"Not up there, Whitney," rasped Talbot. "I'm sure they know that most of my men are quartered down at the T-Bar. Which means they plan on using the northern route." Then he told his *segundo* to send someone back to

130

his ranch and bring the rest of his hired guns, spare horses and at least a week's provisions, that he planned to leave at first light for Celia Farnsworth's ranch. "Damnit, the telegraph office up to Greybull is probably closed. But first thing in the morning I want a wire sent up there alerting my men to the situation."

With the departure of Whitney, the cattle baron could barely contain his vengeful rage. By not coming here, Talbot figured, the ranch woman was defying him. Of course, Moses Quinta had put her up to this! He should have let Whitney gun Quinta down when the opportunity had presented itself here at Silver Springs. And also by not appearing, Celia Farnsworth had spurned Talbot's love.

"She has to pay for this," said Talbot as he reached over and grasped his cane while lurching up from the chair. A crazed look in his eyes, he lashed out with the cane, a backhanded blow that swept the flickering candles and bowl of flowers from the table. "Both of them have to pay!"

Westward the spiny ridge of the Rockies gnawed like grizzly's teeth at icy blue light spreading across the sky, with the cavalcade of riders from the T-Bar Ranch riding through pockets of shadow still clinging to the basin. They'd been in the saddle coming onto two hours, the lodestar which they'd been guiding by fading away as the sun appeared from behind the Big Horns and set to gleaming the snowy peaks.

To the hired guns, working for a man like Charlton Talbot was a shade better than dodging the bullets of a posse after robbing a bank or Wells Fargo stage. Their bellies were full, the pay was good and what law there was in the basin took orders from the cattle baron. It augured well with them, too, that they were going to unlimber their guns against a smaller force. Some of these men had lustful turns of mind, and having caught a glimpse of the ranchwoman's daughters down at Silver Springs, a few minutes alone with these girls would be to their liking.

"About another mile," Tex Whitney called out to the cattle baron over the thudding of hoofs and creaking of saddle leather. "How do you want us to handle this?"

Holding up a restraining arm, Talbot and his men came to a ragged halt, where they squinted at the rancher seated with the sun at his back, the harsh sunlight haloing Talbot's face filled with smoldering hatred and cynical arrogance. And though their faces were shadowed by the brims of their hats, their eyes were those of killers, of the wolf pack waiting for the signal from its leader. None of them would trade this moment for a full house or a week's drunk down in Denver, and the rancher sensed this as he spoke.

"We'll split into two groups. Tex, pick the men you want. And if there's any resistance, use your weapons."

Wheeling his horse around so that he faced the others, Whitney motioned to those men to his left that they would ride with him, then he twisted to glance at Talbot. "We'll work our way around to the north and come in that way. Move out!"

On their way toward the ranch buildings, the men with Charlton Talbot spread out more and reached for their rifles. Day had come fully upon the basin to reveal the empty corrals, which further confirmed Talbot's suspicions that Celia Farnsworth's herd was on the move. While some of the riders jumped their horses over the

132

encircling fence, the rest along with the rancher clattered in through the open gate, and as Talbot drew up by the wind tower, his men rushed inside to search the buildings. He had the gut feeling that everyone was gone, and the bitterness he felt toward the ranchwoman intensified when those who'd been searching the house blundered outside to tell him that it was empty.

Cursing, Talbot shouted, "Burn everything to the ground!"

Pitch tar was found at the blacksmith shop. They smeared it upon hunks of wood, then they separated to touch flame to the wood and hurl the burning pieces through doorways or shattered windows, some of them caught up in the frenzy of what they were doing and mouthing rebel or Indian yells. Almost immediately the hip-roofed barn became engulfed in flame as did the smaller, wood-walled buildings. Smoke billowed out of ranch house windows before tongues of fire could be seen.

Pow, pow!

Talbot responded to gunfire coming from the north by reining in that direction, and then he saw Whitney coming over a rise and motioning the rancher to head that way. "Let's move out!" shouted the rancher over the crackling of burning buildings, the reflecting flames showing the grimacing smile on his face.

When he reached the elevation where Tex Whitney was waiting, Whitney said, "You were right about her heading up north. That trail they left is an open highway."

"How much of a head start do they have?"

"Couple of days at the most."

"Then we've got them," Talbot said viciously.

"You stand to make a big profit out of those cattle."

"I'm seeking more than profit, Whitney. Quinta and the others must be killed."

"I reckon Mrs. Farnsworth took her daughters along. What about them, and her?"

"She had her chance," he said grimly. "What I'm saying, Whitney, the men who ride with me stand to hit it big. With her out of the way, and maybe some of the other ranchers if they pool their herds with hers, it'll only be a matter of months before I control the entire basin."

"I always did have a hankering to own a hunk of land."

"That could be arranged."

"Reckon I'd better prime myself for some killing," the *segundo* said eagerly, and together they spurred along tracks left by the 77 cattle.

14

The cattle seemed to move of their own accord into a canyon through which Shell Creek flowed, to follow canyon walls rising sheerly to either side and showing layers of sediment and the blacker streaks of lignite. Creek water boiled around sunken rocks and boulders, and the banks were thick with underbrush, aspens and willows grown big as trees. The onrush of cattle flushed up coveys of sharptails and flocks of lesser birds took wing from trees. The men handling the herd knew their business as did the cutting horses they rode, and more likely than not when a steer cut away from the herd or made a move to break back to the mouth of the canyon, it was the horse which made the initial move of working the steer back with the other cattle. The lowing of cattle, or hands whistling shrilly or shouting to keep the herd moving down-canyon, echoed off the rocky walls.

Some distance in front of the herd were Zach Lankford with his string of pack horses and Celia Farnsworth's daughters, at the insistence of Moses Quinta. If danger came, he'd told Celia and the other ranchers, it would be in the form of the cattle turning back upon themselves once they were up in the pass or of Talbot's hired guns catching up with them.

Back on the slope of a hill about a mile from the canyon, Quinta brought his field glasses to bear upon a column of smoke coming from the general direction of the 77 ranch buildings. Passing the glasses to Ben Tygee, he flicked ash from his cigar down at the rock-littered slope and asked, "How long do you figure before they'll be here?"

"We passed through some rugged country, Moses," deliberated the rancher as he looked through the glasses. "But these men will be pushing their horses hard." He handed the glasses to Quinta, removed his hat and used the same hand to swipe at his brow. "I figure they'll be here sometime around nightfall."

"That should give us enough time to get the herd up into those mountains."

"We're not that far from Greybull," pondered Tygee. "And it could be that Talbot sent a wire up there."

"I wouldn't put it past him. Still, Ben, that wire would have been sent from Silver Springs, telling his men up north to keep watch for our cattle."

"That cattle baron is damned foxy. Just supposing he figures us to go up Granite Pass. That being the case, Moses, we could have company sooner than we expect it."

"Things have been going too smoothly at that, Ben."

"We've got you to thank for that. It sure sets well in my mind you being here." And in a sly aside, the rancher added, "Been noticing, too, that Celia has taken a shine to you. Be a fine woman to team up with."

Grimacing, Quinta muttered, "Just thinking of getting hitched after all these years of lonesoming it gets me to itching all over." He turned his horse after Tygee's. "For now, Ben, let's keep that fire to ourselves. Stubborn as Celia is, she might ride out after Talbot."

Ben Tygee nodded, and then he said, "A damned shame burning a person's life work to the ground. Talbot's got to be stopped one way or the other."

Easing their horses off the slope, they cantered toward the herd still pouring into the canyon, the quartering wind sending dust billowing toward the southeast. Some distance in front of the herd, Zach Lankford and the girls were coming onto rocky spires guarding the lower reaches of Granite Pass. On the canyon floor there was no wind, but coming strong to them was the murmuring of creek water. Another turn in the canyon brought them onto hard, gravelly ground rising into a mountain track, the sight of where they were going to ride causing the plainsman to utter reassuringly, "Once you're up there it don't look so high."

"I hate this—this doing nothing," protested Beth Farnsworth.

"What we're doing is scouting ahead."

Amanda swung her pinto around. "Come on, Beth, let's go help work the cattle. You stay here, Sara."

"Now lookee here, girls!" shouted Lankford after Beth and Amanda riding back into the canyon. "Stubborn as mules, just like their ma." He spat down at the track as he glared at Sara. "Don't you be getting no ideas either."

"I like scouting better," she said impishly.

"Doggone if you ain't one Farnsworth woman with some common sense. Lordy be! You sure you ain't no orphan?"

"Nope, Uncle Zach, I sure ain't."

Celia Farnsworth's reaction when she saw her daughters coming around a bend in the canyon was to

137

lash the ends of her reins down at the shoulders of the black, the horse doing a prancing sidestep as it fought the bit. But Celia couldn't spur ahead because of cattle bunched up against the south wall of the canyon. She was riding alongside Hank Willard, who spoke around a rueful smile.

"Got grit, them girls."

"They'd get more than that if I could get up there!"

"Simmer down, Celia," he said calmly. "Your daughters are better horsemen than a lot of hands I've ridden with. And some smarter, too."

"Don't pacify me, Hank Willard. They're damned disobedient, and you know it."

"Well, Mrs. Farnsworth, once they get hitched, their husbands can straighten them out." He waved his coiled riata at cattle turning around, then spurred ahead and got them pointed the other way.

"I'm not sure I approve," said Celia as she moved up to Willard, "of the young man Beth is seeing."

"Yeah, Raoul Dixon? Sometimes youngsters don't put too much stock in their parents' opinions."

"I just can't bring myself to trust Dixon."

"Well, he came back," said Willard as Quinta and Ben Tygee rode up.

"See anything?"

"Just a lot of prairie," responded Quinta. "It's around noon. Think I'll head out of the canyon and find me a high spot. By now a lot of folks have seen our trail dust, including some of Talbot's men. If I spot any riders coming in, I'll signal by firing twice."

"Be careful, Moses."

"Always am." Quinta flicked a finger against the brim of his hat and reined his horse around, still thinking about that look he'd seen in Celia's eyes. Though her concern had been for him, her fear of what was to come showed plain on her face. And Quinta felt a little uneasy too. If Charlton Talbot and his men caught up with them, Talbot was certain to order his men to use their weapons now that Celia hadn't kept that appointment down at Silver Springs. By not showing, she'd spurned his love. Quinta could still recall the lust he'd seen in Talbot's eyes, and nothing short of killing the cattle baron would stop the man.

About an hour later, the entire herd strung out in the bending recesses of the canyon, Ceila Farnsworth got her first glimpse of Granite Pass. The sight of its massive rock contours heaped and stacked as though by an underground eruption and climbing the mountain wall brought a moment of alarm. There was a track or game trail going up it, the plainsman had assured her. But this first breathtaking view of the pass summoned up that old fear of what had happened to her husband's father. She could feel the slight tremor when she placed her hands over the pommel. "Steady," she whispered, wondering if Tygee and Willard had seen the moment of weakness. Then Celia's worry of what they intended to do passed to another problem that had been troubling her as she spotted Raoul Dixon and her daughter, Beth, riding together.

Raoul Dixon pulled the bandana away from his mouth as he spurred close to Beth Farnsworth, the sting of the choking alkaline dust getting into his eyes and nostrils. "You and Amanda were told to head up into the pass!"

"Raoul, I can handle myself."

"Some of these cattle are getting a little spooky," he said curtly. "I can't tend to them and worry about you at the same time."

"You mean you actually worry about me?" Beth asked stingingly.

Dixon pulled the reins out of her grasp as his horse sidled and hammered about and snorted through flaring nostrils, with its eyes rolling in their sockets. He slapped a hand against its neck to quiet the sorrel down, and then Raoul Dixon nodded at where Tim Petrie and Amanda were working cattle deeper in the canyon.

"You see, Señorita Farnsworth, Tim is afraid to leave Amanda's side because of his fear that something will happen." He loped both of their horses along the moving flank of the herd as the outrage of what was happening to her showed in Beth Farnsworth's eyes, flashing resentment, and the dawning knowledge, too, that once they reached Sheridan she would ask Raoul to marry her.

"Amanda," Raoul Dixon said sharply, "I want you girls to vamoose up that pass. Pronto!" He tossed the reins back to Beth.

"You'd better do it," said Tim Petrie.

"Tim, this isn't fair!"

"Fair ain't got nothing to do with it, Amanda," he came back.

Glaring at Dixon, Beth said, "We'd better do like they say, sister of mine. All I can say, Dixon, is that you Spaniards are damned bossy!" Both girls spurred away to be cloaked in the rising dust.

Laughing, Tim Petrie, "Now I sure enjoyed that."

"Once women get the upper hand," Dixon said sagely, "there's no living with them."

"You speaking from experience?"

Dixon smiled with his eyes. "Something my pa told me."

"You fixed on tying the knot with Beth?"

"Don't know. You?"

"I sure cotton to that Amanda girl. Right now my prospects are slim, Raoul. It'll be pretty hard supporting a wife on a cowhand's wage. But, yup, I done sprung the question."

"Why, you sly fox," retorted Dixon. "All along I've been figuring you for one of them bashful go-to-church types. And all along you've been stealing Mrs. Farnsworth's hens out of her chicken coop."

Then the cow boss, Jud Walker, swung out of the dust and told them to stop jawing and get to work.

When Zach Lankford rode into a narrows, the breath of his brown horse and those trailing coming in jerks, he suddenly realized he'd reach the top of Granite Pass. He let the horses labor up a little higher and onto a track running deeper into the mountain and at an upward angle, but with a clearly defined trail passing through a pine forest.

Sara Farnsworth passed him on her cayuse, a horse a couple of hands smaller than Lankford's, and he called out to her, "Best give the horses a breather." Sliding to the ground, he loosened the saddle cinch and went back and checked the packs on the other horses, while from below came the low bellowing of cattle moving up the pass.

Sara dismounted with the nimbleness of youth and ground-hitched her horse before stepping off the trail to move under the high branches of a ponderosa. The forest floor was littered with pine seeds and cones, and it was a deep brown color. Her eyes went to loose bands of pygmy nuthatches flitting among the branches, and deeper in the forest a group of crested Stellar's jays, feathered in blues so intense that they appeared almost black, scurried about as they searched for insects in the root-choked soil. Under the trees the air had a still, dead feel to it, a sort of musky scent in it mingling with the aroma of pine, and it was cooler on this high plateau.

As Sara moved over to her horse, Lankford trudged back from where he'd taken a look at the pass, and he remarked dryly, "The leaders are about halfway up, Sara girl. They'll sure be a-wanting water when they get up here. Which means that stream I run into about three miles thataway."

"It's sure peaceful up here." Sara climbed into the saddle.

"It be that, alright. Game's plentiful, too."

They passed on, with Sara Farnsworth out front and following a trail made by game animals and widened by others like Zach Lankford who'd ventured into the Big Horns for solitude or to kill an elk or deer or grizzly.

Coming into a clearing, Sara smiled at hummingbirds swarming beelike around the trumpet-shaped blossoms of scarlet gilia, their wings making a continuous chorus of shrill, clicking sounds. The trail crossed the small meadow before filtering into forest again and angling off to the northeast. Beyond the screening trees there seemed to be nothing but more mountains, their slopes steep and heavily timbered at the base, then covered with frost-split and sliding shale. In passing through the clearing, sunlight lanced down at them, with the ground squelching as the horses moved through icy slush.

Mingling with the deep green of evergreen trees were stands of aspens wearing autumn gold.

When they reached the stream feeding into a marshy pond, Lankford let his horses slake their thirst. "When your horse is watered," he said, "tie him over in those trees. It'll be a good place to make camp."

"How long will it take them to get the herd up here?"

"If there's no trouble, Sara, another two, three hours. See them blueberry bushes down by the draw? Be nice to have some for supper. Come along, now, and I'll rummage around in my packs for a pot. Then you can get to picking."

A couple of hours after Quinta had settled down on an elevation giving him a clear view of a vast section of the basin, a wind seemed to come out of nowhere. He'd spread his sheepskin over a flat-topped boulder and elbowed down on it, one of the seventeen-shot Winchester .44 rifles he'd gotten compliments of that storekeeper back at Laramie close at hand, the unblemished sun warming the rocks around him. Now a sudden gust of wind snapped coldly at his face. The northwestern horizon, he'd been noticing, was going a hazy gray color.

"It'll probably snow tonight," he murmured.

Fortunately there'd been no snow on the pass, but Quinta had the nagging feeling that lady luck was going to leave them. Six or seven inches of snow could bog the herd down in those mountains. It would also serve to keep Talbot's hired killers from heading up the pass. But this wouldn't stop the cattle baron, since Charlton Talbot knew that if those ranchers pooling their cattle could defy him, others would try.

Again he used his field glasses to scan the rugged approaches to the canyon opening onto Granite Pass. This was lonely and tedious work, made more so by the presence of the chilling wind. Pushing to his feet, he moved to his horse and pulled a bottle of Red Dog out of a saddlebag. He drank sparingly, with the whiskey hot in his mouth and warming in the belly before it spread like flames licking at underbrush. The cigar tasted better too now, but the thoughts of what a snowstorm could do to this high plateau country crinkled his eyes into worry lines. It was a good thirty miles across the tops of those mountains, and up there, you brought the cattle along slowly, your worry more on gaping ravines or sudden dropoffs than on Talbot's hired guns.

Quinta's rangy black tossed its head before nudging at his arm and nickering nervously, and hurriedly Quinta shoved the bottle back into the saddlebag and eased down to look over the rim of the high precipice. Then he spotted seven riders coming from the northwest, using a coulee as their route toward the canyon. They rode like men out for a Sunday morning constitutional, letting their horses amble along, or like hands out hunting for stray cattle, but revealing itself through the prism lenses of his field glasses were the faces of men used to killing, revolvers snugged down low, the T-Bar brand riding at the hips of their horses. One of them tossed off a joke, and a couple of the others laughed sardonically, but their eyes remained cold, watchful, mirthless. Quinta judged them to be about three miles away, and now when the horsemen emerged from the coulee to find the long flank of a foothill, the lowering sun at their backs pushed mile long shadows ahead of them.

Already Quinta had judged that the hired guns would

have to ride beneath the prow of the height he was on once they crested that other hill, and at a range of three hundred yards he could do a lot of damage with the Winchester. Some of the tension drained from him now that a little shooting was in the offing. In prison, he'd learned that patience was a sort of virtue, but sure as sin there wasn't anything virtuous about what these hired killers intended doing, and it was Quinta's plan to separate these men from their saddles by the simple procedure of downing their horses. Others with less experience would go for the riders, hard shooting under any conditions. Afoot, he'd found out from past experience, too, a man wearing high-heeled boots didn't have the gumption to walk long distances.

He snugged the rifle stock against his chin and brought the barrel to bear on the hats of the lead riders bobbing over the summit of the hill, and kept it there as all seven horsemen came down the eastern slope, those at the point riding three abreast, the four trailing spread out more. The only shelter on the hill was some mesquite bushes and small boulders, and though the hired guns could see the mouth of the canyon, they still rode sloppy in their saddles.

At a distance of around four hundred yards, Quinta sighted in on one of the horses, followed it for another hundred yards, then pumped four quick shots at that horse and the others in front. As the agonized squeals of the horses mingled with the startled shouts of men being thrown out of their saddles, Quinta managed to bring down two more horses before the remaining pair of riders could make it back over the hill.

A slug ricocheting off the boulder he was crouched on brought Quinta's rifle swinging back to a man standing over his dead horse, and anger glinted in Quinta's eyes as he snapped off a shot that caught the man in the stomach. The hired gun staggered backwards, doubled up as though he'd been hammered in the middle by a massive blow, then he pitched forward to lay spread-eagled and face down. The other hired guns broke running back up the hill, and Quinta helped them on their way by firing near their churning legs.

Ruefully, Quinta drawled, "Maybe I done wrong by not killing them. But I ain't sunk so low as to backshoot a man yet."

Quinta rode his horse along the ridge line until he came to a cut which gave him access to lower ground. Then he headed at a gallop for the canyon, his mind turning to Talbot and those other riders coming from the south. In all probability they wouldn't be here until nightfall, and even Quinta, despite his reckless nature, wouldn't make the climb of Granite Pass after dark. But he was almost certain that Talbot and his men would make that climb.

Once he was in the canyon, Quinta went at a slower gait in following its bending rock walls, and then he reined up when four riders came galloping toward him. Among them was one of the ranchers, Kiley, who shouted out, "We heard gunfire."

"Ran into some of Talbot's men."

"How many?"

"Seven men—those, I figure, who Talbot sent up the the Lazy M." They began riding deeper into the canyon, with the top of Granite Pass coming into view, where some of the other hands were working the tail end of the herd and chasing stragglers back with the other cattle. They rode into shadow cast by a wall and several rods later moved single-file into sunlight striking the mountain track. After their horses had labored up to a level spot, the rancher drew up and glanced over at Quinta.

"I don't doubt that they'll be after us," remarked Kiley.

"Well," said Marv Sundeen as he cast a speculating look at the northern horizon, "it's coming onto snow, if I read sign correctly."

"Yup, it's sure getting colder."

"You get two, three inches of snow on this pass," Kiley said, "and a rider'll play hell getting a horse up here."

"You're right about it going to snow," said Sundeen. "My knee has been acting up ever since high noon."

"Maybe the reason for that, Sundeen, is that around noon was the closest we came to them saloons over to Greybull."

There was some subdued laughter, and then Quinta said, "For sure it's going to be a cloudy night. Windy, too. Which should help Talbot's hired guns if they make a serious attempt to come after us. And I'm a-thinking they will. Come nightfall, we'll take turns standing watch."

"That makes sense to me, Quinta. 'Cause we sure don't dare move the cattle through these mountains at night." Then the rancher, Kiley, accompanied by a couple of hands, continued on up the pass, leaving Moses Quinta riding alongside Marv Sundeen.

"I'm itching to get some of those killers in my gun sights, Moses."

"Got a light?" asked Quinta as he pondered briefly over just to why he'd let those hired guns live. Without a shred of doubt they would have gunned him down from

147

ambush, and left him stripped naked for the vultures to find, to boot. But it was a tactical error he'd have to live with.

"Reckon I do," said Sundeen.

"That being the case, have a cigar."

"Imported," Sundeen said around a smile. Striking a wooden match against his belt buckle, he cupped his hands around its flickering flame and lit his cigar, and then Quinta's. Moving on, the wind coming at them stronger now, and with the deeper moan of what was to come behind it, they remained silent as their horses went carefully upward, their shod hoofs dislodging pebbles that tumbled away.

"Got something to say, Quinta, and I don't want no argument about it." Under the shadowy brim of his hat, Marv Sundeen's steady gray eyes found Quinta's. "Me and Ed Pratt will camp out up near the top of the pass. I figure that damned cattle baron owes us for what he done to our boss. Some of the other hands are married, got yonkers. Wouldn't be fair to them having to swap lead with them hired killers."

At the moment there was nothing Moses Quinta could say, and they kept on the move until at last they'd come into the pine forest of the mountain, and here Quinta told Sundeen to head for night camp and get something to eat and his bedroll. As the hand clattered away, Quinta brought his horse under the trees and left it there, and with his Winchester in hand, he moved down and made himself comfortable where he could see the pass dropping fast below and the sweeping reaches of the canyon and the land beyond. Snuggling deeper into his sheepskin, he soon lost himself in the melancholy of his reasons for being up here in the Big Horns.

15

The ragged column of horsemen poured down the slope and pulled up to form a half-moon circle around a campfire flickering on the bank of one of those nameless creeks cutting through the Big Horn Basin. The men who'd been hunkering there came uncertainly to their feet as Charlton Talbot reined closer to the fire. Through sullen blue eyes Talbot looked past the six men at the pair of horses standing under a yellow tree.

"Well, what happened?"

"We was bushwhacked!"

"Your horses, where are they?"

"Shot out from under us."

"There must have been five, six of them waiting in ambush."

"No!" the cattle baron said harshly. "It was Quinta!" Although the men by the fire could see anger impale itself on the pasty folds of Talbot's face, it was the crazed glimmer in the man's eyes that silenced them.

Even the *segundo*, Tex Whitney, was troubled by Charlton Talbot's inability to control his temper. Talbot, the *segundo* mused bitterly, is consumed by his need to get back at Celia Farnsworth. They wouldn't be here now if he'd been allowed to gun down the gunfighter back at Silver Springs.

They'd ridden hard, and would have to push their horses some more if they wanted to get up in the mountains before it started snowing. The wind coming out of the northwest had that damp, heavy feel it always got during a weather change. In the fading light Whitney gazed worriedly at the clouds that were passing overhead, churning and rolling as they passed, and they were dark gray and heavy with snow. He could still see the vague humps of the foothills, but the mountains beyond them were hidden behind the plane of clouds. The horses, not wanting to face the penetrating wind, were trying to swing their hindquarters to the north, while those astride them had the look of men who'd rather squat around a warming fire than keep after the herd. Some of them weren't as fit as working cowhands either, having fleshy faces or rounded bellies, and with their bodies aching from the long hours they'd been in the saddle. A few, however, had staying power, with the *segundo* figuring the reb, Turk Oldham, to be one of these, along with Palegro, a half blood out of Sonora, and it was Whitney's intention to let these two men lead the way up Granite Pass.

Spurring his horse ahead, Whitney drew abreast of Talbot's black thoroughbred, where he said, "Once we get into that canyon opening onto the pass we'll be out of the wind. But it won't hurt none to let the men warm themselves around this fire."

"I'll say what we do!" replied Talbot. "We're moving out. We brought along extra horses. You men—" he gazed back at those standing around the fire—"get saddled up. You should be able to catch up with us by the

150

time we reach the canyon." He brought his black around. "Let's ride!"

With little difficulty they rode over the wide track of ground churned up by the herd, and then a wall of snow poured out of the clouds as night also pressed down upon the basin. The chilling wind fell away when they clattered into the canyon mouth, with the cattle baron out in front and setting a loping pace for the other riders. Nearly an hour later, by the *segundo*'s estimation, Charlton Talbot slowed his horse to a walk, and then all of them were straining to see Granite Pass through huge billowing flakes forming a white curtain between where they were riding on the canyon floor and the mountain. When the wind let up, the snowfall parted a little to show them that the storm had dumped a couple of inches of snow on the gravelly track they would have to climb. And now, even the cattle baron knew it was time to rest the horses, and he dismounted stiffly. Saddle leather creaked as the others stepped to the ground. The whickering of horses wanting a drink was muffled by the falling snow, and the breath from both men and animals was coming out thick as churned milk. Behind Talbot's hired guns were some pack horses and the string of spare horses.

Above the canyon walls Tex Whitney could hear the heavy throat of the storm, but where he stood by his horse it seemed peaceful, with the pale light of night enabling him to see ground objects up to fifty yards in the distance, bottles of whiskey being passed around by the men, the faint glow of cigarettes. Those who'd wintered in this northern plains country before set about tying leather thongs around the cuffs of their pants to keep the snow and wind out or putting on extra clothing and tying their hats down with scarfs—these men were craving comfort, not style. For the unwary it would mean frost bitten ears or worse.

The *segundo*'s attention passed to the cattle baron, who stood apart from the others while staring up at the pass. Somehow Charlton Talbot seemed indifferent to the deepening chill of night, to the danger that lay ahead, even to the snow dusting his sable cap and heavy mackinaw coat. When the six hired guns they'd encountered back in the foothills appeared out of the whiteness, Talbot swung around while blinking a faraway glaze out of his eyes.

"They'll be waiting," he said.

Around a nod the *segundo* said, "Reckon so. It's kind of calm down here; but up in that pass the wind will play hell with the horses."

"A thousand dollars to the man who guns down Quinta."

"I'll pass the word along, Mr. Talbot." Then Whitney stared up past the shoulders of his big sorrel at the white, smoldering shape of the mountain bending over them. "It could storm for two, three days. Which means that herd could get stranded up there."

"I don't give a damn about the cattle."

The harsher inflection of what the cattle baron had just said told the *segundo* that they were to leave no survivors, and for the first time in years Whitney felt a stir of conscience. Though right now he'd give a month's wages to have Moses Quinta in his gunsight, gunning down women went against his grain of thought. But if he hesitated or showed any signs of uncertainty, others here were chomping at the bit about taking over as *segundo*, and still another unmarked grave would be found in this canyon.

152

"You get my drift, Whitney?"

"I'll pass the word about that too," he said tautly. Reaching for the ground-hitched reins, he brought his horse in among the hired guns, and curtly he relayed the gist of what the cattle baron wanted done to the people they were after.

"You figure them damned ranchers will be waiting up there?"

"What you're getting paid to find out," responded Tex Whitney. "Oldham, you and Palegro take the point."

"Si," came back Palegro, a wiry man with watchful black eyes and a hooked nose. "I know much about these mountains—where there is water, game . . . and the ones we want." Fastening a sardonic smile for the *segundo,* he climbed aboard his horse and rode after Turk Oldham.

It was much colder on the middle reaches of the pass, the wind reaching out for the men and their horses, the icy pellets of snow seeking exposed flesh and riding out of a grayness in which no clouds were visible. The snow-sodden track had become slippery, and the hired guns had been forced to dismount and walk ahead of their horses. The falling snow was heavy with moisture; it clung like wet plaster to the backs of the horses and formed icy ridges on their eyelids and around their flaring nostrils. At the level places Talbot and his men were forced to wait for several minutes, fighting to get their wind back, and waiting for the horses to stop quivering from the cold as they used what grass they could find to rub the caked snow away from the back and mane of each mount. The branches of the few pine trees on the pass sagged under the heavy weight of this new

153

snowfall, and some of the men sought shelter under some of them, but mainly it was the thought of what was to come, the killing, that brought them on the move again.

Each cautious step Turk Oldham took with his spurred boots brought him higher on the track. The snow he labored through was piling up more, forming finger drifts extending outward from boulders or trees, the few bare spots showing black. Under the sheepskin and extra clothing he'd donned, Oldham was perspiring, and tiring also from the effort he'd put into the climb. A few yards behind him was the dim form of the half blood, Palegro, who'd been whistling one of those Spanish sonatas while he climbed, mouthing curses whenever he slipped and dropped to his knees in the deepening snow.

"Hey, Oldham, a nice night for a walk!" shouted the grinning Palegro.

Turk Oldham flung over his shoulder, "You damned greasers are plumb loco!"

"Careful, my friend, how you speak," said Palegro.

A sneer split Turk Oldham's lips that had been compressed together because of the cold wind pounding at him while he attempted to drag more air into his aching rib cage. But the epitaph he meant to throw back at the half blood went unspoken as a lead slug slammed into his right cheekbone and tore the life out of him in passing through his skull to explode out of the back of his head, and the hired gun sagged lifelessly into the snow. The scent of Oldham's blood came to the bronc. It reared backwards and neighed its fear before stumbling down the track and into Palegro's horse, with both horses tumbling into the snow. Somehow the half blood managed to evade their flailing hoofs as he threw himself behind a small boulder. Clawing out his revolver, Palegro

154

tried to locate those who were firing down at him, then he cursed when rifle slugs found Oldham's horse, peppering snow into Palegro's eyes from where he lay belly-down on the ground.

Further down the track, a hired gun screamed his fear when a bullet found his midsection, and as he dropped out of the saddle, his right foot got wedged in the stirrup. His frightened horse bolted down the track, dragging the screaming man.

Talbot's men let their horses go as they sought shelter. The heavy reports of the rifles continued for a few minutes, the echoing reports being snatched away by the storm, along with the receding sound of the horses heading downslope. When the rifles cut out, Tex Whitney was the first man to come cautiously to his feet. His eyes surveyed the mountain above, then swiveled to the cattle baron coming erect.

Holstering his revolver, the *segundo* said curtly, "You willing to listen to what I've got to say, Mr. Talbot?"

Charlton Talbot forced down his anger over what happened as he brushed snow from his clothing. He was breathing heavily, more from his fear than the climb up here. "We're still going after them!"

"It wouldn't look right to your men us turning back now," Whitney agreed.

"Well, out with it."

"If this storm keeps up, that herd will get bogged down up there. And we sure as hell won't be able to get our horses up this pass. I'm suggestin' that we camp down in the canyon. Maybe in two, three hours, we send up about five men on foot. There was maybe three rifles up there. Our boys shouldn't have any trouble killing those men, then using their horses to go after the herd and stampeding it to hell and gone over that mountain. It'll take them ranchers at least a week to gather their cattle again. Meanwhile, come sunup we ride south for Powder River Pass. Once we're over the Big Horns, we cut north and be waiting when them ranchers bring that herd down the eastern slope. It should be a turkey shoot, Mr. Talbot."

"Your plan has merit," Talbot said quietly. "And for certain the snow is getting too deep to bring our horses up Granite Pass again."

"I'm suggestin', also, Mr. Talbot, that the men get some bonus out of this. Sloppin' around in these mountains in this kind of weather just ain't to their liking."

"Yes, this would serve to reassert my authority," he said haughtily. They fell into step, the hired guns moving downhill with them. "That damned Quinta has won this skirmish—but I'm confident victory will be ours."

"You still want them women taken care of?"

"Without question, Whitney. That damned territorial judge over at Sheridan is a stickler for law and order. Which means we can't afford to leave any witnesses behind."

And then the cattle baron waved his men closer to speak with a smug confidence. "I'm giving you men an extra's month pay for what you did tonight. If this storm doesn't kill those ranchers, I'm confident your guns will do the job."

Huddling under his blanket, Raoul Dixon forced his eyes open when a glowing cinder crackled out of the campfire and drifted up with smoke filtering through the boughs of the ponderosas. The blizzard still raged over the mountain forest, a heavy moaning wail of wind and the lower creaking of trees. He was restless, curiously remote, as if his thoughts were far removed from where they were camped near to top of Granite Pass. This same restlessness had caused young Dixon to picket his cutting horse deeper in the forest and away from Pratt's and Sundeen's horses standing under trees fringing onto the trail which led up from the pass. He couldn't shake the feeling that despite the danger of trying to travel up the pass in this weather, the cattle baron would have his men make another attempt. Talbot's hired guns were expendable, and maybe they were too, pondered Dixon, as he turned sleep-filled eyes upon patches of snow that had formed on the forest floor.

"Time," he said, removing the blanket from around his shoulders, "to take another look at the pass." Shoving the blanket into his bedroll, he picked up his Winchester. Hefting it in his left hand, he swung quizzical eyes to where his horse was picketed as it whickered nervously, and Dixon crouched under some branches and moved that way.

Pow, pow, pow!

Raoul Dixon groaned under the impact of a slug catching him in the side and catapulting him to the ground just beyond the screening branches of the tree. The heavy hammering of rifles continued as he managed to scramble to his feet, unaware that he'd dropped his rifle. Trailing blood, he plunged through knee-deep snow and managed to untie the reins from where they'd been looped around a thick branch, with the sorrel jerking its head up and trying to buck. A bullet fired by one of the ambushers nicked Raoul Dixon's shoulder, and desper-

157

ately he flung himself behind a fallen tree, his horse breaking free and pounding away.

"I got this one pinned down over here!"

"The others are dead. Don't let him get away, Palegro!"

Quickly Raoul Dixon scrambled backwards on his hands and knees, and then he rolled behind a ponderosa. Lunging to his feet, he started running, forgetting the wound at his side, the bullets fanning air around him.

"Over there!"

"Damnit, he's heading downslope!"

Despite the agonizing pain coming from the bullet wound and the fact that he was weakening, Dixon kept on the move, with the forest opening up more as he came onto it fringing onto the high edge of the mountain, and with the ground rock-littered and covered with deeper snow. Without warning, he found himself stepping into space. There was no time to scream, to have rise in him a sensation of terror, as he fell while twisting around and trying to clutch for some support. Then the hard impact of landing on a rocky ledge some twenty feet below the edge of the cliff knocked the wind out of his lungs, and he felt no more.

Sometime later the sound of voices brought Raoul Dixon out of his stupor, but when he managed to blink his eyes open it was to find that he was covered with snow. The sudden arm movement when he reached up to brush the snow away from his face caused him to gasp in pain. Only then did he realize that standing above him on the cliff edge were those who wanted him dead.

"Yup, Palegro, he sure enough took a walk into space."

"Good. Since there are four of us and only two horses,

we must ride double. Once we find the herd, we'll use our knives on those guarding the remuda. Then we'll stampede the herd."

"Just leave one of them Farnsworth women to me." The man laughed cruelly. "I aim to get me some lovin' before I slit her pretty lily-white throat."

The one called Palegro laughed and said, "Until then, keep your pants buttoned up, *amigo*. Let's vamoose."

And Raoul Dixon muttered grimly, determinedly, as he fought to rise from the snow, "I must get back there . . . warn them. . . ."

On shaky legs, he unbuttoned his sheepskin and removed a leather glove. Then his probing fingers examined the wound; he discovered, to his intense relief, that the bullet had come out through the exit wound at his back, and the bleeding had stopped. He tore a piece of bandana away and used it to plug the wound. For some reason he felt better, but there was still the problem of working his way up to the plateau above. He slipped on his glove and stepped along the narrow ledge until he found a crevice curling upward, and dragging air into his lungs, he started to climb, with each new handhold causing a wave of dizziness. But the thought of the one he loved finding herself at the mercy of those killers kept Raoul Dixon moving up the crevice until at last he was crawling over the edge and coming into a shambling walk that brought him upslope and into the pine forest again.

He followed the tracks left by those who'd pursued him back to the campsite. The bodies of the other hands were still wrapped in their bedrolls. A terrible rage burned its way into Raoul Dixon's mind when he leaned over and closed Marv Sundeen's eyes. But this was not the time for vengeance, rather that of clear thinking. The herd was at least five miles deeper into the mountain, and since the trail was probably blocked by snow, going there on foot would be almost impossible. The only chance he had was to find his sorrel, which he'd trained to respond to his whistle. Pausing long enough to pull Sundeen's Winchester out of its scabbard, young Raoul Dixon slipped northward through the screening branches and began searching for his bronc.

16

It was the thick silence that caused Moses Quinta to lift the hat from his face and peer up at Douglas firs forming a solid green roof over where he lay in his bedroll Around him were the forms of others still gripped with sleep. He tossed the blankets aside and shoved to his feet. Stepping to the edge of the trees, he gazed at the deep snow in the clearing and on the trees blotting up sound in a velvety quiet, before realizing that the eastern sky was paling into sunrise. Though scattered clouds still hung over the Big Horns, he could feel the power in the wind wailing high over the trees, with a sudden gust scudding up snow from the clearing and swirling around Quinta. Dimly he could discern a nightrider walking his bronc through the cattle bedded down in the clearing and in other clumps of trees—some of them sounded off as they realized the blizzard had about run its course. And Quinta also welcomed the glow of Zach Lankford's campfire across the clearing and under trees lining the creek. But close at hand and under the trees, the horses they would use today were standing quietly.

The craving for a hot cup of coffee brought Quinta back to his bedroll, which he rolled up and tied behind his heavy Texas saddle. Then he picked up the saddle and saddle blanket and moved over to his horse, which seemed to be staring intently, deeper into the black maw of the trees.

"Easy," Quinta murmured as he crouched to see under the branches. There were plenty of brown bear up here, or it could be a passing elk. Briefly, he wondered if some of Talbot's men had managed to make it up the pass, but Quinta discarded the idea as he began saddling the bronc.

He rode southward along the fringe of the clearing. When he came to a gap where the trail running over here from Granite Pass ran across the clearing, he searched westward along it for any sign of tracks. All he could see in the new snowfall was an angling track left by an elk, though the three men who'd been watching the pass should have returned before this, and Quinta carried the worry of this over to the campfire.

"Yup, Moses, Sundeen and the others should have been here by now," agreed Jud Walker. "Or they could be waiting for first light."

Nodding, Quinta asked, "When do you figure on getting the herd started?"

"Sometime this morning, I'm hoping. But this snow is deep, Moses."

"We'll have to bring them along slowly."

Ranchers Bill Kiley and Ben Tygee rode up and tied their horses under the trees before settling down at the campsite, along with three hands who'd been keeping watch over the cattle. It was still shadowy under the trees where they were gathered, the air having the cold snap of night to it, and with snow lying thick along the flowing waters of the creek. Now that they had weathered the storm, they were content for the moment to share an easy camaraderie while having a breakfast of side pork and gravy over biscuits washed down with chicory coffee, and that black and thick. The aroma of the coffee, the more heavy scent of cigarettes, and of Quinta's cigar, came acrid into their nostrils, and then Ben Tygee brought up talk of the cattle baron.

"That storm kept Talbot's men from getting at the herd," he said.

Then Bill Kiley said in that clipped voice of his, "Knowing how downright ornery Talbot it, I figure we ain't seen the last of him."

"Maybe not," said Walker, "but getting the cattle up Granite Pass is something to be proud of. Well, boys, here comes Celia and her daughters." And by unspoken accord the men turned the subject of their talk to what the price of cattle would be at Sheridan. As Quinta glanced over at Celia and two of her daughters riding single-file through the trees, the distant whickering of a horse resounded where the remuda was gathered in just past some pine trees forming the northern edges of the clearing. But the cattle in the clearing and under those trees seemed more interested in grubbing for foliage in the snow. Out in the clearing, one of the five hands keeping watch over the herd gave his round-rimmed hat a curious tug as he spurred his horse at a walk through the feeding cattle and toward the remuda, but Quinta's eyes had swung upon Celia moving out of shadow and into firelight.

Celia seemed more relaxed as she returned the nods of the men here with smiling eyes. Her eyes flicked to Quinta, who rose and made room for Celia close to the fire, then he went over and bent down to clean the untensils he'd used with fresh snow before handing them to Zach Lankford.

"Well, Zach, how's the lumbago treating you this morning?"

"Got stiffening of the joints for damned certain, Moses. You made up your mind as to where you're heading once we get to Sheridan?"

"Got too much on my mind to ponder over that now, Zach."

Lankford fastened a slow grin. "Woman trouble being one of them worries?"

"For a cook, you're getting mighty uppity," Quinta said softly but with no sting in his words.

"You're even getting to sound like the boss lady," said Lankford as he looked past Quinta at the sight of a sudden burst of sunlight striking Sara Farnsworth and her dappled pinto where she was working her way through scattered bunches of cattle grazing in the clearing. "Lordy be! The sun!"

Turning to look, Quinta's eyes narrowed in disbelief when the sharp crackle of gunfire came from north of the clearing. The next instant cattle were exploding out of the trees. Behind the cattle appeared four horsemen holding revolvers that spouted flame at the terrified cattle, which broke directly to the south, flinging powdery snow skyward.

Immediately, Quinta knew they couldn't make it to their horses, and swinging to the others, he shouted, "Our only chance is to get to those boulders over by the creek!"

"Sara!" Celia screamed. "Don't try to stop them! Ride out of the way!" She started that way, only to be grabbed by Ben Tygee, and with Quinta moving on her other side,

164

they ran through the deep snow toward the rocks. When Quinta turned to look back at the clearing, it was to see Sara Farnsworth's pinto bucking and fighting the bit before it was swept away into a solid mass of stampeding cattle.

Back in the trees beyond the campsite, the horses plunged and leaped and managed to tear away the straps of restraining leather. Freed, they broke into the clearing and swung southward with the running cattle as those with Quinta slipped in among the snow-heaped boulders which were piled precariously along the creek bank. One of the hands moved too deeply among the rocks and found himself breaking through snow edging over the high bank and dropping into the chilling waters. He came up gasping, then two men grasped his arms and pulled him back among the rocks. Now a bunch of around four hundred head split away from the main herd and headed directly for the campsite. The cattle blotted out the fire and came crashing through some of the trees, the spray of snow they were raising sweeping toward the boulders so that those huddled there could only see bits and pieces of cattle.

Quinta sprang upright and pulled out a Peacemaker as he worked his way north among the boulders, and when he spotted the men who were stampeding the cattle, he moved out into the open and toward them. One of the riders saw Quinta, and yelled something to another horseman, and quickly they wheeled their broncs Quinta's way. Dropping to his knees, Quinta unholstered his other gun and waited calmly for the oncoming riders. Then Quinta's right gun bucked three times, with the front rider stiffening in the saddle before spilling into the snow, his horse veering sideways and bolting after

165

the cattle.

When a slug tugged at Quinta's hat brim, he threw himself onto his side, rolled over and came up firing. Though Quinta's first bullet missed, he scored hits with the next two. As the hired gun sagged and grabbed for the pommel while trying desperately to raise the barrel of his Smith & Wesson, a slug from Quinta's gun tore into his forehead, and even as the ambusher was toppling backwards over the haunches of his bronc, Quinta had grabbed the reins and was swinging into the saddle.

Leathering both guns, Quinta brought the horse out of a frightened buck and managed to head it at a gallop after the stampeding herd. As he rode, Quinta knew the hired guns had come up Granite Pass, which would explain why Sundeen and the two hands with him hadn't come back. That would be three more names added to the list of men Charlton Talbot was responsible for killing. And, too, he would hold himself responsible if something had happened to Sara Farnsworth. To bring Sara's broken body back to her mother would break Celia's heart, and break, also, this thing that had sprung up between Celia and him.

"You always did have a way of setting your sights too high," Quinta scolded himself as he came to a bluff, where he reined up hard.

The bluff sloped gradually into a mountain valley in which the cattle had split into scattered groups, the run gone out of them now as they drifted to find shelter or water. Quinta figured it would take at least three days to gather up the cattle and head them back toward the trail. Then he used his field glasses to scope the valley for any sign of Sara's pinto. There was a resurgence of anger over what had happened when he glimpsed around fifty head of cattle lying motionless beneath the sheer edge of a cliff further to the east. Then Quinta almost dropped the glasses when a gun sounded. Turning his horse to the west, he managed to shove the glasses back into a saddlebag and spur away from the slope while staring at two riders who'd suddenly emerged from a tree line. Quickly, he reached down for his rifle, levered a shell to arm it, and from hip level fired at the hired guns. One of their horses staggered, then its front legs buckled, with its rider vaulting out of the saddle. The other horseman cantered his horse around and vanished back into the trees as Quinta's horse leaped forward.

The man on the ground had dropped his rifle, and realizing that he wouldn't be able to pick it up in time, he made a frantic grab for his holstered gun. The heavy crackle of Quinta's Winchester resounded a split second after a leaden slug slammed into the man's rib cage, and he was dead before his body fell into the deep snow. At the tree line, Quinta stilled his impulse to go after the other hired gun as several riders topped a rise and veered toward him. Casting a bitter glance at the dead man, Quinta rode to meet the riders.

"They scattered the remuda to hell and back," said Hank Willard.

"How many of our men did they kill?"

"Benson, who was watching the remuda, had his throat cut from corner to corner—and Shorty Graves got gunned down."

"It could have been worse," Quinta rasped out as they came to the slope opening onto the valley, where they reined up to study the lay of the land below. "No sense waiting until the others get mounted. We'll have to split up and work our way in a line down into the valley."

167

"I'm just hoping Sara isn't hurting too badly," said Willard.

"Yeah, well, let's do it," Quinta said grimly.

Counting Quinta and the rancher, Willard, there were eleven men, and they spread out while letting their cutting horses pick their cautious way down the slope. They had to go slowly because of the deep snow, and the knowledge that there were hidden pockets under the snow which could conceal Sara or her pinto. Though their hopes were high, all of those searching for Sara Farnsworth knew that the harsh reality of the situation dictated that if they found her at all, she would be dead. This thought accompanied Moses Quinta as he moved down into a section of valley tapering toward the southwest.

An hour passed before other riders appeared on the rim of the slope and came down to help in the hunt for the missing girl. Then it was noon, and still the search went on, with Quinta's eyes going occasionally to Celia Farnsworth riding about a mile to the east of him. He'd talked her into bringing her cattle up here, so the responsibility for what happened lay in his hands, and right now an embittered Moses Quinta wouldn't have wanted it any other way. This was the last herd that Charlton Talbot's hired guns would ever stampede, because Quinta was determined to kill the cattle baron in cold blood. There'd be no waiting for the man to draw, or for his hired guns to give Quinta a fair chance, and if he died in the attempt, Quinta reckoned that was the way the cards were meant to be cut.

Sometime in the afternoon, Quinta brought his tiring horse into still another stand of timber through which the cattle had run. The cloud cover had gone away and the warming sun hung low to the southwest in a clear sky. The days had gotten shorter, but there was still a good three hours of daylight left. However, if they didn't find Sara today, Quinta doubted she could survive a night out in these cold and dangerous heights.

Suddenly he came across hoof marks left by a horse, and the weariness went away. As best he could, Quinta followed the tracks, only to pull up sharply upon encountering a rocky bluff, and upon peering over it, grimaced when he saw the pinto sprawled on some rocks at the base of the slope, a good twenty feet below where he sat in the saddle. Below him, too, were scattered pine trees, and the hope flared in him that Sara could be holed up among them. But when he glanced again at the dead horse, the way its neck had been broken, and estimated the distance it had fallen, he came to the sickening conclusion that Sara Farnsworth's body must be covered with snow, and wearily he dismounted.

Crouching by the rim, he eased over the edge and slid to the bottom, where he examined the pinto before scanning the immediate area for Sara's body. Beyond the rocks upon which the horse lay, the ground slanted up sharply into a series of humpbacked ridges dotted with more pine trees, while the draw he was in cut away to the west. Quinta worked that way in a stumbling walk through knee-deep snow, helping himself along by grasping at branches. It was tiring work, his progress impeded by his sheepskin and high-heeled boots, and as Quinta lunged forward to grab the branch of another tree, he was almost certain he'd heard the nearby rustling of other branches, and he looked around wildly.

"Well, Mr. Quinta, it took you long enough!"

Quinta stirred up snow as he spun in the direction of Sara Farnsworth's voice, and the biggest smile he'd framed in many a year split his lips when he gazed upon her huddled under a tree, and he plunged toward her to slip under the branches and enfold the young girl in his arms.

"Oh, girl, girl," he murmured, while to his surprise, Quinta found himself kissing Sara's tearstained cheeks, and that his own eyes were misting.

"You're . . . hurting my arm . . . Quinta," Sara gasped as he eased away. "I—I think it's broken."

"Sara girl," he said tenderly, "don't worry. Old Moses here is an expert at setting broken bones. Are you sure there ain't nothing else wrong, girl?"

"Just that I'm thirsty—and cold."

"Shucks, I done forgot my canteen—" Quinta nodded toward a sheltered place further down the draw—"but I'll sure enough make a nice fire in there." He eased out a revolver, and holding it away, he triggered off three shots.

"You know, Mr. Quinta," she said, "everybody thinks you're a big, bad gunfighter. But you know . . . you're nothing but a . . . a big softie."

"Word gets out about this," he said in mock sternness, "and my life won't be worth a plugged nickel. OK, just crawl out from under there—that's it, easy now."

"You seem to like my ma a lot, Quinta—"

"Don't start with that kind of nonsense now, girl." He brought her into his arms. "I've got enough trouble now that your ma's cattle are scattered all over this valley."

"You do, though."

170

"Some," he admitted. "But your ma won't hear it from me."

"You know, despite all that's happened, I like the mountains."

"Sara, girl, don't be a-saying that to your ma, or for certain she'll tan your breeches." Then they shared a quiet laughter, and a deeper awareness of one another, and now Quinta felt a certain sadness, for in getting to know Sara Farnsworth better, it would be just that much more difficult to say his goodbyes when they reached the railhead at Sheridan.

They saw each other about the same time, Raoul Dixon drawing rein first on the frozen trail, and eastward the hired gun, Palegro, just rounding a bend and shaping a sardonic grin as he stopped his horse. Right away Palegro knew he had the edge if it came down to gunplay, and his attitude was almost fawning as he said, "Hey, *amigo*, how goes it?"

Raoul Dixon just sat there, ignoring the throbbing of his wound, but at his side Dixon's numbed fingers were arranging themselves around the curved butt of his double-action .45.

And around the words the half blood was throwing at Raoul Dixon issued a clucking noise to which Palegro's horse responded by stepping along the trail.

"You looking for the herd?" went on Palegro in that same snaky-calm tone as if he'd just offered to buy Raoul Dixon three fingers of tequila at the local cantina. He kept on gesturing disarmingly with the hand holding the reins, the right hand resting casually on the pommel but

171

only inches from the holstered gun riding high on his hip. Though he was tired, and wanted nothing more than to make tracks off this mountain and head for the saloons over at Worland, the half blood wore a patient smile, with the dark brown eyes seeming to contain no malice. Halting a couple of rods from Dixon, he gestured at the snow-laden trees towering over them.

"*Si, amigo*, such pretty country up here. But we were talking about the herd."

There was a blurred crooking of Palegro's right forearm back and down toward the ivory-plated butt of his revolver, which he palmed and whipped out of the holster to the crackling report of Raoul Dixon's double-action .45, and Palegro's forehead creased away from his disbelieving eyes. The impact of the slugs tearing into his belly and chest caused the half blood to rock in the saddle. Dying, he muttered, "Hey . . . *amigo* . . . ," choking blood through a grimacing smile.

Raoul Dixon stopped firing only when the hammer clicked on an empty chamber, and the damning hatred he felt for the half blood turning his face ashy and slitting his eyes.

For a moment the revolver hung on Palegro's trigger finger as he gazed at the bullet holes in his coat and the blood seeping through to stain it, then the spark of life went out of his eyes and he fell out of the saddle. In wheeling around, one of the bronc's shod hoofs slammed in Palegro's head and crimson flared as the scalp was torn away.

Raoul Dixon watched the horse wallow through a huge snowdrift to come out onto the forest floor and then go crashing through some pines in its frenzied attempt to get away from the smell of death and dislodge the saddle clinging to its back. The silence after the horse was gone, and after the hammering of his gun, stretched so long he began to get jumpy. Dixon stared uptrail, figuring that more of the hired guns would happen along, then remembered that he'd emptied his Colt double-action, and with cold-numbed fingers he refilled the chambers. Thrusting his gun into the stiff holster, he leaned over the neck of his horse, more tired now than he'd been before, and trying to will strength back into his muscles.

The hired gun had as much as told him that the herd was scattered over the mountain. Maybe if he hadn't spent all that time trying to find his horse and tried to walk out he could have warned the others. And what about Beth, was she still alive?

Reining his horse over to some low branches, he scooped snow into his hand and held it to his mouth to suck the moisture out of it while heading up the trail. Somehow he could sense the presence of the other hands, Sundeen and Pratt, and bitterly he threw the handful of snow away. They deserved more than to be gunned down by Talbot's scum.

When Dixon was still out on the trail he could see the glow of the large campfire, and when he came to the clearing, he stopped and studied the way the stampeding cattle had chewed up the snow and torn branches from trees. Suddenly he realized that those gathered around the fire were looking in his direction and that two horsemen were loping toward him with drawn guns, and with the night shadows giving way to a deeper blackness.

"It's Dixon," one of them said.

He recognized the graying hair of Ben Tygee under the

173

cattleman's hat, and the bigger rider as being Moses Quinta. Pressing his arm to his wounded side, Dixon swung further into the clearing and toward them. They put their guns away as Dixon said bitterly, "They hit us early this morning when I was standing watch. So I figure it's my fault Sundeen and Pratt are dead."

"You hurt bad?"

"Nothing I can't live with, Mr. Tygee." Slowly Raoul Dixon drew out each painful word in his telling of the ambush. "And just about an hour ago I rode into one of them heading toward Granite Pass."

"A half blood?" inquired Moses Quinta.

"Yup. Figured he was real cool—and had me measured. But I pumped five shells in him before he had a chance to talk himself out. But—but it still don't make amends for what happened . . . to the others."

"We'd best get you over to the fire, Raoul."

"What about the cattle?"

"Lost a few head," said Quinta. "Figure it'll take us a couple of days to round them up. And they got Benson and Shorty Graves." At the moment, he saw no need to tell Dixon what had happened to Sara Farnsworth as he rode with the others across the clearing and into the trees shielding the campsite. But upon dismounting, he found Celia Farnsworth waiting for them. Quinta let Ben Tygee tell of what had occurred at Granite Pass.

"Come morning, Celia," said Tygee, "I'll send a couple of men up there with pack horses to get their bodies. I figure they deserve a Christian burial."

"They would still be alive," Celia said stonily, and through embittered eyes, "if we hadn't sent him up there!"

174

"Aren't you being a little hard on the boy?" said Tygee.

Celia's eyes never left Raoul Dixon's drawn face. "Dixon, I can't prove that you're still drawing blood money from Talbot. But everything sure as hell points that way. When we get to Sheridan, you're through. One more thing, Dixon: stay away from my daughter or so help me I'll kill you!"

17

At first light they'd traversed Powder River Pass, and now the Big Horns lay behind them, with the settlement of Buffalo a dark huddle of buildings beyond the foothills. The sun was still flushing cold orange over the horizon, while the sky was clear and an icy gray color. After they passed through patches of snow melting on a gentle hillock, the stagecoach road drummed hard when their tired horses clattered onto it.

Tex Whitney and the cattle baron rode abreast out in front of the hired guns. Just before they'd broken camp this morning, Charlton Talbot had promised that they would rest up at Buffalo before heading out again, and Whitney was mulling over this as a log cabin fell behind on his right. Money bound these men to the cattle baron, but from the complaints the *segundo* had overheard during the long haul over the mountains, the majority of those here would foresake a summer's wage just to hightail it the hell away from this cold country, and in a way Whitney couldn't blame them. These men were used to hitting hard and fast, then spending their ill-begotten gains a shade faster on loose women and games of chance. They weren't long-haulers.

During the time he'd been *segundo* out at the T-Bar, Whitney had kept his distance from those he bossed. He considered himself a cut above these men, and for certain of better stock than the cattle baron, who Whitney didn't trust either. Once Celia Farnsworth and the other ranchers with her had been killed, their ranches would be up for grabs. And Tex Whitney had the notion that Talbot wouldn't let him have any of his land, despite the man's promise to him. He'd taken a shine to Celia's 77 Ranch, and was still angry that Talbot had allowed his men to destroy the main buildings.

"Damnit," muttered Whitney as he stabbed a glance over at Talbot riding slouched in his fancy saddle while breathing heavily through his mouth, "you're just a no-account southern redneck who got lucky. Them fancy clothes," went on Whitney in barely audible tones, "cover a body gone to seed—and your mind's warped too." Whitney figured that Palegro and the others who'd gone up Granite Pass had perished in the storm. But they'd done it for the money, which was all that kept him and the other hired guns on the T-Bar payroll. But Talbot's promise to him that he could own some land had caused in the *segundo* a mind change. He no longer wanted any part of this wandering life, of hiring out to scum like the cattle baron, who was a bigger thief than him or the others here. So when they got to Buffalo it was Tex Whitney's intention to have the cattle baron sign a piece of paper confirming that promise, or for certain he'd turn the hired guns against Talbot.

Now they cantered along a street lined by log cabins ad clapboard houses hovering under cottonwoods, the newly fallen snow covering debris littering the barren yards between the buildings, the sun rimming the eastern horizon to set to sparkling the snow on the peaked roofs. Whitney led the way onto the wide, downsloping Main Street, where a drummer standing alongside a gaudily painted two-wheeled cart with big red lettering on it in front of Warner's Livery Stable paused in his clumsy attempt to harness the black horse hitched to the cart and glanced curiously at the heavily armed men riding past. By unspoken accord the *segundo* swung his bronc toward the Elephant Bar showing light through its grimy front windows. Eagerly the hired guns tied their mounts to the tie rails and trailed in behind Whitney and the cattle baron.

As Charlton Talbot settled down at one of the tables, Whitney strode across sawdust covering the floor to the long bar strung along the west wall. The waves of heat coming from the potbellied stove brought up the stale beer and tobacco scents. While some of the hired guns fanned out at the bar, others found tables, but they let the cattle baron sit by himself, with three of them moving back to where a shabbily clad man was sleeping on the pool table and blowing snores through his walrus beard. Unceremoniously two of the hardcases grabbed the sleeping man's arms and legs and carried him over to toss him out through the back door being held open by their companion. Racking the balls, and finding some cues and chalk, they began playing a game of rotation.

Over at the bar, Tex Whitney drank thirstily from the bottle of Four Roses whiskey, and lowering the bottle, he said, "Any sign of that T-Bar herd?"

"Passed through yesterday afternoon," responded the barkeep from where he stood behind the row of brass beerpulls. He was heavyset, with a few strands of black hair crossing his scalp, and he had on a faded white shirt

179

and red sleeve garters. "Camped up north a couple of miles. Should be pulling out for Sheridan this morning."

"This town big enough to have a barber?"

"You betcha."

"Then send the other barkeep for the barber. Mr. Talbot is craving a shave."

"You mean . . . have him come here?"

When Tex Whitney got to drinking he could be mean, and more than once he'd hammered someone into the sawdust for no good reason, but eating at him was his suspicions that he was being used by the cattle baron, and Whitney rasped out sourly, "Either you ain't woke up yet or you're addle-brained. And my men are craving some vittles; have some steak and eggs brought over too."

"Cer-certainly." He went over and relayed what Whitney wanted to the other barkeep, who scurried out from behind the bar without bothering to remove his apron and went out the front door.

One of the fixtures in the saloon was an upright piano placed back along the east wall, and Tex Whitney grimaced when discordant jangling notes began coming from it as one of the hired guns banged away at the keyboard while trying to play an off-key rendition of — "Buffalo Gal."

Half-turning, the *segundo* fixed his slitted eyes and displeasure on the cattle baron. Every night the men had been ordered to set up Charlton Talbot's tent, a cumbersome bundle of heavy canvas and rope ties, and while Talbot had been sleeping under the comfort of fur robes out of the biting cold and wind, his men had braved the elements in their bedrolls. There'd been room in that damned tent for four, five others, and it still rankled

Whitney that as *segundo* he hadn't been invited to sleep there. He recalled, also, that Talbot had been hovering at his right elbow when a bonus had been offered to Palegro and three other men if they would trek up Granite Pass and stampede the herd. Then, after those men had started up the pass, he'd happened to glance at the cattle baron, and a shudder of fear had run through Tex Whitney after he'd glimpsed the blank glimmer of indifference showing in Talbot's eyes. At that moment it had been plain to Whitney that the cattle baron didn't care what happened to the four men. And if Talbot could order his men to gun down Celia Farnsworth and her daughters, Whitney's own life was just as expendable. Somewhere along the way, Whitney realized, the last shred of human decency had left the cattle baron, that the man's one driving compulsion was his crazed notion of turning the Big Horn Basin into his own personal cattle empire.

"Yup, he's sure enough crazy," muttered Whitney as he braced himself with more whiskey. Then he swung away from the bar and went over to the cattle baron's table

Whitney sat down without bothering to remove his hat. He'd worked himself into a bitter mood, so he merely nodded to acknowledge Talbot's curt smile. "I ain't gettin' any younger, Mr. Talbot."

"None of us are, Tex. Something seems to be bothering you."

"It won't be too much longer before a lot of land in the basin will be up for grabs. And I aim to file on some of it."

"I would be disappointed if my *segundo* was a man without ambitions. What do you have in the way of collateral?"

"Come again?"

181

"Money, Mr. Whitney. In order to buy land one must have hard cash."

"Reckon I've saved up some."

"That's commendable. And I do remember, Tex, my promise to you that you'll acquire some land."

"I want that in writing, Mr. Talbot."

Charlton Talbot laughed easily, softly. Reaching into an inner coat pocket, he produced a large black-leather wallet from which he extracted a folded piece of paper. "I was anticipating your asking about this," he said pleasantly. He passed the paper to Whitney, who unfolded it.

"Well . . . now, I ain't too good with reading—but I recognize my name right enough."

"And I'm hoping, my signature at the bottom. The gist of that agreement merely states that I'll help you in buying a sizable chunk of land in the basin. Is that agreeable to you, Tex?"

"Why, Mr. Talbot," said Whitney beaming, "it sure enough is."

"So you see, Tex, my cattle empire does include places for my friends." He extended his hand to Whitney, and his *segundo* shook it vigorously as he shoved up from the chair.

"Listen up!" Whitney said around a wide grin. "I'm buyin' a round for the house. So everyone belly up to the bar!"

As Charlton Talbot's hand closed around the shot glass, his eyes filmed into hard black agates, for that piece of paper he'd just given to Tex Whintney was the man's death warrant. Inwardly the cattle baron was smiling, but it was a bittersweet smile of a man who had no friends, and wanted it that way. Once he solidified his hold on the basin, those who still lived there would come begging for his support. Then he could buy the friends he needed, or anything else that he craved.

"A pity Celia is so stubborn," he murmured. "More a pity that she has to die." But Celia Farnsworth had stood up to him, and though he still had strong feelings for the woman, she'd consigned herself to a mountain grave when she hadn't shown up at Silver Springs. "Damn her, anyhow!"

Of all the men gathered at this campsite midway between Buffalo and Sheridan, the latter town lying fifteen miles to the north and on the eastern flanks of the Big Horns cloaked in alpenglow as night settled on territorial Wyoming, it was Charlton Talbot's opinion that only one of them, a working hand named Pat Zachery, qualified to be his new *segundo*. But in order to get the job Zachery would have to kill Tex Whitney.

There were two fires, Talbot and Dill Liscomb's working hands gathered at one, the hired guns at the other, with five of them engaging their whiskey-laden minds in a poker game. Before leaving Buffalo, Talbot had stocked up on whiskey, dispensing most of it to the men who'd be riding with him to Granite Pass. He'd agreed with Tex Whitney that the best place to ambush the ranchers would be when the cattle were coming off the pass.

"You did a good job with my cattle, Bill. Seems to me they gained some weight on the drive."

Around the cautious smile touching his eyes Liscomb said, "It was touch and go when that storm hit, Mr. Talbot. My men deserve the credit for getting the herd through."

When Talbot and his men had showed up just before sundown, Bill Liscomb could tell that their horses had been ridden hard. And he'd overheard one of the hardcases bragging about what they'd done to Harley Luger's H-Bar-L herd, and of how they were after another herd that had been taken up Granite Pass into the Big Horns. Back in '84 he'd ridden for the H-Bar-L, and now that Luger was dead by order of Charlton Talbot, Bill Liscomb firmed up his decision to quit working for the T-Bar. He'd gone beyond the point of anger, and Liscomb lowered the rim of his hat over his eyes to conceal from Talbot the emotions playing across his weathered face. His bitter eyes staring into flames fanned by the quartering wind, Bill Liscomb knew that he'd be no better than those hired guns if he gave in to this impulse to draw his .44 Colt percussion and kill the cattle baron.

"Mr. Talbot," he finally said, and cuttingly, "I'll get your herd to Sheridan. But after than I'm calling it quits." He shoved to his feet.

Rising, Talbot stared across the fire at Liscomb. "If it's a question of more money . . ."

But Bill Liscomb had already tossed his cup down and was striding toward the picket line. Fastening a smile for the others still at the fire, Charlton Talbot went the opposite way, around the chuck wagon and toward where his tent had been pitched by some underbrush screening the mouth of an arroyo snaking off into the darkness. The moon was full and melony, hanging high to the southwest, with moonlight outlining the humped backs of the mountains. The soft lowing of the herd bedded down about a half-mile further north came to Talbot, as did the chatter of the hired guns clustered around their fire. He crouched, into his tent, only to emerge through the back tent flap, where he hurried into the brush. He worked his way deeper into the arroyo, and coming onto its bottom, moved toward the dark figure of Pat Zachery seated on a boulder.

"I hear you're pretty good with a knife," said Talbot as the waddy struck the tip of a wooden match across his belt buckle, then brought the flaming match up to light his cigarillo.

"Some folks brag on that," Zachery said matter-of-factly.

"Good enough to take care of Tex Whitney?"

A sneer split Zachery's bloodless lips, and he muttered disdainfully, "No problem, Mr. Talbot. But you'll be needing a new *segundo.*"

"Kill Whitney and the job is yours." Quickly the cattle baron detailed to Zachery how it would be handled, and then both men moved back toward the campsite, but with Zachery circling around and over to where his horse was picketed.

Back in his tent, Talbot touched flame to the wick of a coal-oil lantern. A bottle of imported brandy lay on the portable cot, and he was reaching for it when Tex Whitney tossed the tent flap aside and entered. "Didn't mean to take you away from the poker game, Tex."

"No problem, Mr. Talbot." He smiled as the bottle was passed to him, and after taking a long drink, he handed it back. "Brought our horses. But what's so important that we can't talk about it here?"

"Let's just say, Tex, that I'm a cautious man when it comes to discussing business ventures."

"Yup, reckon I don't trust a lot of the scum you've hired on either." Whitney went out first, and both men climbed into their saddles and rode in the direction of the herd.

"First, I'd like to discuss tomorrow's battle plan. The hired guns will go along with my orders to kill the women."

"That bunch," Whitney said scornfully, "ain't got no feelings. They're worse than the Blackfeet when it comes to lifting hair, too."

"I want no survivors, Tex."

"There ain't gonna be none. Been wondering too, Mr. Talbot, about that land I'm gonna get. Been sorta fancying the 77 spread."

"Consider it yours, Tex."

They drew rein about forty rods from the dark mass of the cattle spread over several hundred acres as one of the hands riding night watch veered toward them. Closer, Whitney could see it was Pat Zachery, and in greeting he flicked a finger against the brim of his hat.

"Been hearing good reports on your work, Pat," he said. "When I get my ranch operating maybe you'd hire on."

"Hell's bells, Tex, you've got gypsy blood; no way you can settle down." Zachery laughed with the others.

"The cattle seem peaceful," commented Talbot.

"Maybe so," murmured Zachery as he kneed his bronc forward to come behind the standing horses of Talbot and Whitney. "But I'd better get back to nursemaidin' them afore something spooks them."

Easing the hunting knife out of its supple doeskin sheath and swinging his horse closer to the unsuspecting Tex Whitney, Zachery whipped his right hand over the man's mouth as he jabbed the steel blade at the exposed back. The blade penetrated at the approximate location of the kidney, the intense pain coming from the wound killing the scream in Tex Whitney's throat. Suddenly the body went limp, with both men holding Whitney in the saddle. Talbot managed to grasp the reins and quiet down Whitney's bronc. After folding the upper part of the body over the mane of the bronc, Zachery used his riata to secure it in the saddle.

Talbot found Whitney's wallet, and from it he extracted the piece of paper he'd given to the man back at Buffalo. He tossed the wallet to Zachery and said, "Dispose of the horse, too, Zachery."

Ghoulishly the smaller man pocketed the wallet. "Just leave the rest to me."

Charlton Talbot waited until the other horses had vanished, then he cast an ominous glance at the Big Horns. "Well, Mrs. Farnsworth, tomorrow is your day to die!" And spurring around, the cattle baron brought his horse at a walk back to the picket line.

18

"Maybe you're right, Jud, that the spirits of Indians are responsible for this good weather."

Cow boss Jud Walker had just told Moses Quinta that the unseasonably warm weather they'd been having ever since the storm died out was due to the ghosts of Indians dancing around an ancient medicine wheel located in this part of the mountains. Southward, the sun hung behind Cloud Peak, with Quinta and Walker riding through shadow on its northern reaches and where the trail cut to the east, Their immediate concern was the threat of avalanches, for far above them snow clung to sheer cliff faces, and it was piled deep at the timber line and down into the pine forest of the mountain.

Quinta rode ahead through a narrow gap which had granite on both sides, and pines bristling down the cliffs from clumps of grass and dirt on sheer ledges where they had fallen from high up and clung desperately. Beyond the gap, Quinta slackened the reins and let the grulla pick its own way along a wide ledge over which a mountain wall towered. Beyond this the track brought them into another small valley that had peaks stacked up on all sides of it. The valley was lush with timber, bear grass and creeks eddying through it, with Quinta pondering that there seemed to be no end to the mountains, and he voiced this to Walker.

"Two more days at the most and we'll be over them," Walker replied.

"Coming onto dusk," murmured Quinta as he twisted in the saddle and squinted along their backtrail to where the front of the herd was flowing along at a cautious walk, with Zach Lankford and his pack horses well out in front of the cattle.

Jud Walker thrust aside a snow-laden branch of a Douglas fir as he rode into some trees, where he swung to the ground. "Good place to make camp. Might's well rustle up some firewood."

Quinta dismounted and grinned at the other man. "Why this sudden ambition, Jud? All the cowpokes I know hate to do manual labor."

"Well," Walker flung over his shoulder as he bent to pick up a fallen branch, "I've discovered that Lankford's cookin' improves considerable when he don't have to do all the camp chores."

"Now that you mention it, our cook does seem more human of late." Quinta used both hands to break a limb from a fallen tree.

"Could be that you're right about Talbot and his bunch waitin' for us when we come off the mountains."

"He can't afford to let us deliver this herd in Sheridan, Jud."

"Maybe so. I figure he'll deny sending those hired guns up here, too. Maybe we should send someone ahead to Sheridan to alert the sheriff about what's going on."

"I doubt whoever we send will get through," Quinta said curtly.

190

"Yeah, reckon so. Damn Talbot anyhow for all the sufferin' he's caused."

Under starlight the herd filtered into the valley to spread out in its search for water and grass. There'd been some snow melt, and under the trees and out in open spaces black patches of barren ground showed like stalking night creatures. The wind had died down, the campfire keeping back the encroaching chill.

Quinta had just brought the horse he'd ride tomorrow, a rangy black, over to tie it to the picket line, when Beth Farnsworth came up to him, and a glance at her face revealed a troubled young woman.

"Moses," she said hesitantly, "I need your . . . help."

"That being?"

"Mother is wrong about Raoul. He isn't spying for Talbot. She's—she's blinded herself to the truth, Moses."

"Do you love Mr. Dixon?"

"Enough to run away with Raoul when we get to Sheridan."

"Well, you're old enough to do that, I suppose. You know, though, that Celia and me ain't been on the best of speakin' terms ever since Sara got hurt. But I'll sure enough palaver with your ma on your behalf, Beth. There's something else I've got to tell her too." He reached over and touched Beth's cheek, his smile bringing one to her face. "Just remember, your ma's bark is worse than her bite. Celia's whole life is centered around her daughters and the 77 spread. I reckon I'd be edgy too if someone wanted to drive me off my land. So, Beth, maybe all of us should give Celia a little rope."

"My mother is awfully fond of you, Moses."

"Maybe about the same fondness she attaches to

191

her horses."

"A little more than that, Mr. Quinta. You know, for a gunfighter, well, you're a kind man."

"Gal, my reputation—" he grimaced—"is getting more tarnished all the time. Next I'll be accused of going to church Sunday mornings."

He followed Beth over to the campsite, where trees formed a dark, piny-scent background, and though the moon hadn't put in an appearance, icy chips filled the black dome stretching over the mountains. Supper was over, and under the trees Quinta could see where bedrolls had been placed by saddles, then he turned and looked briefly at Celia Farnsworth seated off to his right and talking to rancher Hank Willard. Sara sat next to her mother. The other girls, Beth and Amanda, were walking with Tim Petrie toward a nearby creek, with the herd beyond and lower in the valley. Still clustered around the campfire were the other ranchers and those cowhands not keeping watch over the cattle.

Quinta had taken his remaining cigars out of his saddlebag, and now he passed them out, saying, "Nothing like a good smoke to mark the end of a long day."

With the toe of his boot Ben Tygee nudged a burning piece of wood out of the fire. He picked it up, lit his cigar, then passed it on so that the others could light their cigars. And in the pale, flickering light Quinta could see the fatigue etched on Tygee's face, who said, "I don't generally indulge in such luxuries as imported Havana cigars. Reminds me, though, of when I was still sowin' some wild oats."

"You mean you done that too, Ben?"

He smiled across the fire at Bill Kiley. "I wasn't always gray-haired and short of wind."

192

Easing away from the fire, Quinta went over to where Celia Farnsworth was making Sara comfortable in her bedroll, and he said, "How's the arm, little girl?"

"The arm," Sara said sassily, "is healing nicely—and I'm not a little girl, Moses."

"For certain I don't see no gray hairs showing."

"Well, Mr. Quinta," Celia said rudely, "what's on your mind?"

"We need to have a talk."

The moon came out from behind a craggy peak to reveal to Quinta the unhappy grooves running down from Celia's mouth, and her eyes were veiled. She nodded somberly and moved deeper into the stand of ponderosas. In a cleared space but with the trees looming overhead, Celia plucked a pine cone from a verdant branch and turned around. "I love the smell of pine," she murmured distantly. "But I still don't like these mountains."

"They take getting used to." Quinta framed what he wanted to tell Celia while listening to the distant yip-yapping of a coyote. Dimly through the trees he could see the yellowish glow of the campfire. Close like this, and with them isolated from the others, Quinta had this strong urge to take her into his arms. He felt awkward standing there, still not certain what he wanted to tell her, and more conscious of the emotions surging to form a tight band across his rib cage. Love, he'd always reckoned, was chiefly a figure of speech. In the past, the only importance he had attached to it was that he'd just love to be dealt three aces in a high-stakes game. But no game of chance had made him so emotionally aware of a woman before, and this despite the fact that Celia Farnsworth had a fistful of faults. Here this ranchwoman

193

was, accusing him of virtually every crime known to civilized man with those big brown eyes, and come tomorrow or the next day he would probably be gunned down by Talbot's hired guns. If he wasn't touched with this loco weed called love, he'd ride out tonight, go back to what he'd been doing before, but what he felt for Celia had already settled the issue.

"I just wanted to say that you've lined out Raoul Dixon all wrong."

"There's nothing to discuss regarding Dixon!"

"Even at the risk of losing one of your daughters?"

"Beth will do as I say."

"Don't figure on it, Mrs. Farnsworth."

"Why is it, Quinta, whenever we get together, we always end up in a fight?" Glaring up at him, she tossed the pine cone away and started to move away, only to have Quinta grasp her arm and say, "There's something else, Celia."

His hand dropped away from Celia's arm. "It's—it's about what Talbot's men did to your buildings. They're gone, Celia—burned to the ground. Leastways that's—"

"Burned?" questioned Celia. "My house? The—the other buildings? You're lying, Quinta!"

"We seen the smoke just before coming onto Granite Pass."

"And you didn't tell me until now!" she shouted, her face going ashy. "Damn you, Quinta!" She came at him with flailing arms and hooked fingers clawing for his face, but he evaded the blows by wrapping his arms around her and drawing Celia close. He could feel her body shuddering under the impact of what he'd told her, and then the tears came.

"Celia, I figured if I told you before, you'd forget about

the cattle and want to go after Talbot."

"You—you knew all this time."

"Yup," he said softly. "And I aim to settle up with that damned cattle baron."

Celia Farnsworth pulled away and said, "He's mine, Quinta! Do you hear, mine!"

Moses Quinta stood there as a shocked and embittered Celia Farnsworth went off alone into the trees. But she left behind her woman scent, with Quinta still very much aware of how it had felt to hold her in his arms. Tugging at his hat, he murmured, "You're wrong, Mrs. Farnsworth. That murdering scum belongs to all of us."

19

Sometime around midmorning the point riders brought the leaders through a small clearing scarred by the rotting timbers of a log cabin, and in the trees beyond they picked up the trail again. The trail was narrow, maybe thirty to forty yards at its widest points, and bunches of cattle were forced to travel among the trees, where the riders had to keep them on the move or they'd stop and mill about in confusion. Every so often on the downsloping contours of this high plateau they'd catch glimpses of the prairie to the east of the Big Horns opening up to them, and with word having been passed by cow boss Jud Walker that they wouldn't noon today.

Zach Lankford and his pack horses were moving well ahead of the herd, and riding with him was Moses Quinta on a dun-colored bronc. "Like I told you, Moses, on this side of the mountains the pass ain't so danged rugged. Should be no problem getting the herd down it."

"Until we run into Talbot's men."

"He ain't the kind to give up," agreed Lankford as they rode across a stretch of barren ground where autumn-touched grass poked through patches of snow glinting under sunlight, and causing both men to squint.

Coming onto a rocky cliff, they dismounted and went on foot up to its crumbling edge. Both men bellied down, while through his field glasses Quinta studied the way the pass sloped along a wide canyon spilling to the foothills. Haze shimmered along the distant horizon. To the southeast Quinta could make out the town of Sheridan, the railroad tracks seeming to split the buildings, some of the chimneys showing smoke lining out with the wind. He scanned the land around the bottom of the pass again, and then sighted up to the rocks near its wide top. "Some snow on the pass," he commented dryly. "Don't appear anybody's ridden through it."

Hawking, Zach Lankford spat tobacco juice over the edge. "That bunch is down there, alright. Which don't help my lumbago none. So, Generalissimo Quinta, what's your battle plan?"

"Mostly, Zach, to keep from going under." He'd run out of cigars, but from force of habit found himself reaching under his coat to his empty shirt pocket.

"Have some chaw."

Quinta smiled the offer away and gazed sunward. "It'll be dark before they get the herd this far. Once the herd is bedded down, the only chance we've got is to have the women watch the cattle while the rest of us slip down the pass—maybe sometime before sunup—and give Talbot's bunch a taste of their own medicine."

"Could work at that."

"I'll talk it over with the other ranchers before I tell Celia."

"She's mule-minded, alright."

"Ornery, cantankerous, opinionated—"

Cackling, Lankford said, "I get the notion you got strong feelings for Mrs. Farnsworth."

"Your cookin' ain't improved all that much, Zach."

"What if they aren't there, Moses?"

"If they aren't, Ben, why, we just ride back up here and bring down the herd. But Charlton Talbot will be there. He's got this crazed notion that Celia done him wrong. That you people have no right to live in the basin."

"He's crazy all right," piped up Hank Willard. "All we want is to live peaceable. But when a man forces a ranch war on you, you got no choice but to strap on the hardware."

In the cooling air of twilight, their spent breath came out in white gusts from where they stood by the picket line stretched between two pine trees. One of the horses tied there, a cayuse with scars showing on its hindquarter, bared its teeth and tried to take a hunk out of the horse standing next to it. The other horses milled about too, and the men knew without voicing it that the horses could have caught a scent borne up by the wind of those hired guns lurking below.

They'd come too far to turn back, with each cattleman clustered in a circle by Quinta knowing that if they didn't get their cattle to Sheridan they would go under. But they stood relaxed, sharing a closeness as of men who trusted one another, men not spooked by shadows or of the hard times they'd known. During the long haul over the mountains they'd been denied the luxury of shaving, and all of them had grown beards. However, their eyes were clear and shining in anticipation of striking back at the cattle baron.

Quinta tossed the rifle he'd been holding over to Bill

Kiley. "That's one of those rifles I got courtesy of a Laramie merchant. It's a Winchester .44 carbine, holds seventeen rounds."

Kiley sighted down the rifle's long, dull-gleaming barrel. "This just might be the equalizer we need against those hired guns."

"Well, you've heard what I want to do," said Quinta. "If anyone else's got a better plan, let's hear it."

"Yours suits me, Moses."

"Yup," said Hank Willard, "there ain't no sense jawing about the withals of doing it another way."

"Count me in, gents!"

The ranchers and Quinta glanced over to find Celia Farnsworth skirting the picket line, and her face set when she came up to them. Forcing a smile, Ben Tygee said, "Maybe it's best you stayed with the herd, Celia."

"You could at least have invited me to this meeting," she chided all of them. "I'm not going to have someone else get killed over my cattle. And like I told you—" her flinty eyes swung up to Quinta's face—"I aim to even the score with that damned cattle baron."

"So you say!" said Quinta through gritted teeth. "We want you and your daughters to watch the cattle when we take off after Talbot. You took me on as your *segundo*. So I'm telling you now, Mrs. Farnsworth, you're staying behind. And I don't want no backtalk about it!"

"It's best that way," broke in Tygee. "Your daughters will need help to watch the herd. Believe me, Celia, I'm not trying to pacify you. Or patronize you, either. But this ain't woman's work. And—and just having you down there would sure worry the sin out of me."

Snow billowed around a horse loping in from the herd ground, and when its rider spotted the ranchers gathered

200

near the picket line, he reined in that direction to pull up sharply by them and dismount at a run. "Seems we lost one of the night riders!"

"What do you mean, lost a hand?" said Willard.

"Four of us were supposed to be watching the cattle. But when I got down to the southwest corner, you know, where that rocky point is, Raoul Dixon wasn't there. So's I rode on to see what happened—but he's gone, I reckon."

"Ain't like a night rider, said Ben Tygee, "to leave the herd without permission. Maybe he got sick and came over to the campfire?"

"Can't you see!" said Celia. "Dixon's been spying for Talbot all along!" She whirled on Moses Quinta. "You brought this on us, Quinta! When we get to Sheridan, you're through." And after ordering the night rider back to the herd, Celia went away.

After a long silence, Hank Willard removed his hat and with the same hand he rubbed the nape of his neck, and said, "Just don't set right with me that Dixon would be in cahoots with that cattle baron. Moses, I reckon we got no choice but to go along with your plan."

Ben Tygee cast a sidelong glance at Kiley, both men telling Quinta that the only chance they had was to head down Granite Pass, and then they went over together to confer with Jud Walker. "We'll head out a couple of hours before sunup," said Quinta.

When the camp had settled down, Quinta sat down by the dying embers of the campfire with Zach Lankford. Among the trees, and where there was some barren ground, Quinta gazed for a moment at the sleeping Farnsworth women. He felt empty of heart, a sort of cold wind hammering at his thoughts, the realization strong in him that it was over between him and Celia. But had there been anything between them except for a strong emotion, and maybe a shared knowledge that had circumstances been different they would have gotten together? She was like the winds that sometimes hit these mountains and the Big Horn Basin, an Alberta Clipper, raging for a day or two and then suddenly vanishing. At least a deck of cards, Quinta thought bitterly, let a man win a hand or two. For Celia Farnsworth was sure enough an unforgiving, cantankerous woman. "Yup," was his silent retort, "give me poker anytime."

"Too bad about Raoul Dixon."

"Just don't figure him taking off, Zach. He's sure earned my trust." He sipped at the coffee as a fiery ember crackled out of the flames and flew up toward the dark growth of trees. "Doesn't make sense him leaving Beth behind, either. A man in love just doesn't act reasonable."

"You speaking for Raoul Dixon—or yours truly?"

His eyes squinting, Quinta muttered, "You sure know how to stretch a friendship."

Most of the saloons and gambling houses were closing when Raoul Dixon rode past the train depot and let his horse pick its way over the ribbons of steel to the holding pens. The cattle weren't used to being penned, and the din of their bellowing kept them stirring about. As he'd expected, there were other brands mixed in with the cattle baron's T-Bar brand. But at least Raoul Dixon knew that the man he'd come to see was here in Sheridan.

Coming down off the pass, it had just been fool luck that he hadn't stumbled upon those hired guns camped in

202

the foothills. A closer look at their camp had shown Dixon a large number of men and horses along with a pitched tent, which he figured belonged to Charlton Talbot. He'd been tempted to pump a few rifle slugs into the tent, hoping that by killing the cattle baron all of this bloodletting would end. But now was not the time for foolhardy acts of bravado. He had endured Celia Farnsworth's tongue-lashing only because of his love for Beth. The ranchwoman would never consent to this marriage unless he could prove to her that he wasn't spying for the cattle baron. In a way, he admired Celia Farnsworth's prideful, haughty attitude, since he considered himself of the same character. And it was because of this that he could never run off to get married. There must be a proper wedding, one blessed by a man of the cloth and the ranchwoman.

Spurring away from the pens, Raoul Dixon rode across the tracks again and onto a dusty street facing the mountains. A dog took to yapping when he passed a brick house shuttered down for the night, and his roan began sidestepping, with a few quiet words from Dixon calming it. He came to an intersection, where a street lamp spilled down lonely, yellow light. He swung onto a wider thoroughfare running parallel with the Big Horns, which carried him southward toward the business section of this railhead town. A few horses idled before those saloons or gambling houses still open, and from them came the tinny sound of piano music. He rode warily, not wanting to be spotted by any of the cattle baron's hired guns, checking the brands of the horses in the street. It was around two going on three, by his rough estimation, with the ride in from the foothills taking him around two hours. Knowing the intentions of Moses

Quinta and the other ranchers to come down the pass before sunup and take on those hired guns increased Dixon's feeling of nervous anxiety.

He swung toward a saloon still beaming light into the street, the Calumet Bar, a log building with a covered porch out front, and he hurried inside. There was one customer at the bar, a drunken townsman with his head draped on his arms placed on the bar top, but three tables were occupied by card players, and Raoul Dixon headed for the back table when he recognized Jake Ramsey, one of the T-Bar hands who'd come in with the herd.

Four other men sat with Jake Ramsey: a fat carpetbagger with grease spotting his checkered vest and grease-tainted hair shining under the overhead lamp, a thin man of sallow countenance and dark clothing who cast Dixon a suspicious glance, another cowhand, and a buffalo hunter, judging from his appearance and sharp aroma. Dixon stepped behind Jake Ramsey and caught a glimpse of the cards the man held, kings over a pair of sevens. Except for the buffalo hunter who'd dropped out, the others tossed chips into the pile in the middle of the table, and when Ramsey discarded one card to be dealt the four of spades, he grimaced his displeasure and glanced back at Raoul Dixon to say, "Heard you had some trouble up in the Big Horns."

"Some," Dixon admitted.

After the carpetbagger upped the ante, the other cowhand tossed in his hand. Ramsey covered the last raise and spread his cards face up on the green cloth. Fastening more of a leer than a grin, the carpetbagger revealed to the other players a heart flush, and with a disgusted sigh Ramsey flipped his cards away and scooped up his remaining chips. Shoving away from the table, Ramsey went ahead of Raoul Dixon to the bar.

"Got just enough left to buy a round," he said.

"Could use one."

"Well, how's tricks, Raoul?"

"It's important that I find Bill Liscomb."

"Could be most anyplace tonight."

"Liscomb was never much of a nighthawk," Dixon came back as the barkeep slid a bottle before them and two glasses and took Ramsey's remaining chips. Hurriedly Dixon emptied the amber contents of his shot glass. "I must find Liscomb right away, Jake."

Downing his drink, Ramsey turned to the other man. He was burly, with ginger-colored hair poking out from under his hat and with a brick-red complexion. "For a fact, Raoul, you look mighty uptight. So let's make tracks for the Rawhider Hotel."

The hotel was located a couple of blocks further downstreet, and in the lobby, their spurs made a chink-chink sound as they passed the counter behind which the night clerk was sleeping in a wicker chair Passing down a hallway, where floorboards creaked under worn carpeting, Ramsey veered over and hammered on one of the doors, then he entered without waiting to be invited inside.

But the room was occupied, by a dresser, some chairs, a wash basin, and a man in the narrow metal bed who'd just sat up and was pointing a cocked revolver at the intruders standing framed in the doorway.

"Oh, Ramsey," muttered Bill Liscomb.

"Easy, boss," said Ramsey. "This hombre's looking for you."

"Dixon?" Tossing the gun on the bed, Liscomb swung his legs to the floor and yawned away his sleep. "From the looks of you, Raoul, you done some hard riding to get here."

"That's right, Bill. I need your help. Yours too, Jake." Raoul Dixon picked his words with care, and after he'd told them just what had happened up in the Big Horns, and his reason for coming here tonight, both Liscomb and Ramsey let the contempt they felt for the cattle baron show plain on their faces, along with considerable anger.

"Count me in, Raoul!" said Ramsey.

"A man can only take so much," Bill Liscomb said as he reached to the chair for his Stetson to settle it over his head. "Being associated with that murderin' cattle baron gives a man a certain stench. Raoul, I can't speak for the other men. But me and Jake will get to roundin' them up right away and back whatever you say." Liscomb's eyes hardened as he added, "A man that will kill women ain't fit to live out in these parts."

20

On the middle reaches of Granite Pass the horsemen scared up a mule deer, which bounded into the broken shadows of trees as Moses Quinta came onto a level spot and stopped to rest his horse. Dawn was a good hour away, and a deep and foreboding silence held sway over the track, with a wintry mist ghosting through the trees and spreading down into the foothills. Quinta more felt than saw the other riders pull up behind him. The storm had piled up huge drifts in the pass, strewn dirt and rocks into them and caked the drifts so that the horses had to struggle through them.

Quinta recollected other times like this, heading out before dawn to do the work of money men, and with him neither asking the reasons why nor caring who he gunned down. Now here he was amidst honest folks in their fight against men he'd called comrades before. He came just short of feeling like a reformed sinner turned evangelist bringing a message of salvation to Talbot and his killers. Only thing was, his message of deliverance would come out of the barrels of his smoking guns.

"Won't be long," was Quinta's bitter comment, "before the devil has some more lodgers."

Moving out of the grayness came Zach Lankford, who said, "Someone's following us."

Shrugging, Quinta said, "Guess there's no way Mrs. Farnsworth will stay behind—or take orders from someone else."

Some of the other riders had turned their horses around and were gazing up the track. The clip-clopping of a horse came faintly to them, faded out for a moment, came again when its rider rode over barren ground, and suddenly Celia Farnsworth rode out of the mist. She pulled up short of the ragged column and sat up straighter in the saddle.

"Like I told you before, boys, I want in on this."

At that moment Quinta had a strong craving for a cigar, a habit he'd always taken to in order to control his temper. He brought his horse along the column and murmured to Jud Walker, "No way she'll go back now. Keep an eye on her."

"I'll do that, Moses. But we'll have to send someone back to help with the cattle."

"It'll have to be Tim Petrie."

Nodding, Walker wheeled his horse back along the track and spoke quietly to Tim Petrie. The younger man's face reddened, and he slammed the palm of his gloved hand down upon the saddle horn before saying something to Jud Walker, and then Petrie brought his horse away from the others and up the track. He passed Celia Farnsworth, and if he looked at her or said anything, Moses Quinta couldn't tell from where he was further below. But he could feel the cold edging inside his sheepskin, and he pulled up his collar while scanning the foothills slowly beginning to take form. Above the looming crest of the mountain bending over him and spreading eastward was a clear sky, the stars in it paling as a pink haze seeped over the horizon.

Maybe Charlton Talbot wasn't lurking below, pondered Quinta, setting his horse into motion, but he was going to ride cautiously, uneasy because of the eerie and windless silence in the pass and Celia's unexpected presence.

When the track widened, Ben Tygee came up to ride alongside Quinta, who'd been using his field glasses to check for signs of movement below and further out among the foothills marred by ravine fissures and a creek snaking to the southeast and in the general direction of Sheridan. Though the ground haze was beginning to lift, the sun seemed hesitant to make its daily appearance. But the growing light set to sparkling the ice-covered trees they were passing.

They drew up on one of the last elevations of the pass, and Quinta looked at Tygee. "There isn't too much shelter down below, not among those rocks."

"It's my opinion," said Tygee, "they'll hit us when the herd is strung out coming onto those foothills."

"That line of trees yonder marks a creek. The place where Talbot would have set up camp."

"Could be, Moses, but there isn't any sign of smoke."

"Hard to tell with all this ground fog, Ben. No sense making like Custer and all of us going down there. Lankford and me'll scout ahead."

"Be careful 'cause there ain't too much shelter between here and where you're headed."

"This old hoss is gonna ride low in the saddle."

"You figure he's got forty, fifty men?"

"I do. The sun being in our eyes don't help matters either. Well, Ben, it's some three miles to that creek.

Bring the others down to that hill."

"The one with that jumble of boulders at its crest—"

"Wait there, Ben." Quinta motioned Zach Lankford to follow him, and then both riders swung their horses down the track.

When they were out of the pass, the sun was starting to poke above the dark land mass making up the north-western reaches of the Powder River Basin, a land once ruled by the Hunkpapa Sioux, now mainly the domain of cattlemen. Their rifles were still sheathed in leather, Quinta's sorrel and the bronc under Zach Lankford starting to blow and sidestep as they walked. The men astride them knew there was danger lurking in the tree line lying some two miles away.

Chiefly, Quinta's concern was for the enshrouding mist still hovering along that line of trees, the crowns of leafless cottonwoods shouldering over willows and sort of floating in the mist. Out where Quinta was riding there was no shelter but for a few scattered piles of rocks and the posts of a fence line which had a strand of rusting barbed wire clinging to them, the legacy left by some sodbuster who'd gone under. And now that old wound at Quinta's side, the one given him by Charlton Talbot, began aching.

"You feel naked as a jay bird, too?"

Around a sudden grin Quinta said, "About. No sense both of us riding in there, Zach."

"This child ain't never shied away from trouble before," muttered Lankford as he stroked his beard. "Anyways, we're coming into rifle range."

"Been noticing that. You don't happen to know any Hunkpapa incantations just in case someone's sightin' down a rifle barrel at us?"

Lankford's eyes sparked into Quinta's, and the old plainsman gummed the hunk of tobacco against his cheek, then he said, "Well, Moses, them Hunkpapa sure swear by that ghost dance—supposed to ward off lead slugs and evil spirits."

"Trouble!" warned Quinta as he pulled up and nodded toward where a flock of birds was winging away from the trees.

This was instantly followed by the heavy report of a Sharps rifle. Quinta heard something slap into flesh, and even as he swung to look over at Zach Lankford, sweeping out of the mist and away from the tree line were Talbot and his hired guns.

"Zach, how bad is it?"

"It ain't good," gasped Lankford, doubled over as he was in the saddle, his left hand pressed against his midriff. He managed to bring his horse around, and took a firmer grip on the reins before spurring his horse into a gallop back toward the Big Horns.

Glancing quickly over his shoulder, Quinta suddenly realized that the hired guns weren't coming hard, but had settled their mounts into a purposeful canter, most of them sitting arrogantly in their saddles, as if they knew that Moses Quinta and the others were already dead men.

He veered closer to Lankford, reached over and grasped the man's arm to steady him in the saddle as a couple of rifle slugs scoured the air over his head. They pounded over a couple of low hills, and at the crest of still another one, Quinta took the reins from Lankford and halted their horses when he saw that Celia Farnsworth was riding toward him, followed by the ranchers and hands bunched closely together.

"How you doing, Zach?"

"Folks who carry guns," muttered Lankford, "generally use them." He straightened some in the saddle, framing a quick smile for Quinta, the pain lines on his face and those glinting in his eyes telling of how bad he'd been hit. "That . . . Celia . . . is sure hell for leather."

"She'll get all of us killed," rasped Quinta.

"We heard shooting!" exclaimed Celia as she reached them. "Zach, you've been hit?"

The other ranchers and cowhands came onto the crest and formed a milling circle around Quinta and Lankford, and as they did so, the sun edged over the horizon, blinding them to what Talbot's hired guns were doing. Then one of the younger hands yelled a warning before Quinta had a chance to speak, and the hand pulled the Winchester out of its boot.

"Spread out!" said Jud Walker. "Mark your target!"

"Celia," Quinta said, "take Zach back to the pass."

"What's this?" questioned Hank Willard in response to several riders suddenly skylining themselves to the east, one of them firing a couple of warning shots.

After squinting into the glaring sunlight, Ben Tygee said, "Why, I'd swear one of them is Raoul Dixon."

"It's Dixon, alright," said Quinta.

Celia spurred forward. "I told you he was working for that damned cattle baron!" she exploded.

"Doesn't appear that way to me," Quinta said as Charlton Talbot and those riding with him wheeled around.

Back on that hill, Bill Liscomb, who had Raoul Dixon riding to his left, said flatly, "OK, boys, you know why we're here. Spread out more as we ride down. But don't be too eager to clear leather, savvy?" At his signal they began working downslope until they were within handgun range. He told his men to halt, and now Bill Liscomb struggled to keep the damning contempt he felt for the cattle baron out of his voice, but the words he flung at Charlton Talbot came out ugly mean. "Your murderin' days are over!"

Pat Zachery let his horse drift away from the other hired guns. He had tried the new handle of *segundo* on for size and discovered that he liked it, though he still hadn't gotten much respect from those he rode with. It had also given Zachery a reckless arrogance, and he blurted out, "What in hell you mean, Liscomb, to come riding in here like this?"

"Yes, Liscomb, you're overstepping your duties!" Charlton Talbot said angrily. "What happens here is none of your concern." His livid eyes slid to Raoul Dixon. "And you, Dixon, you had a chance to make some big money. Instead you sold out to the 77 spread."

"Señor, you have blood on your hands!" Dixon said.

The unexpected presence of Bill Liscomb's working hands had temporarily distracted Charlton Talbot's thoughts from those he'd been chasing. And it had been a long time since anyone had dared speak up to him. He could feel the anger building, and was powerless to put a damper on it because of the intense hatred he felt for Moses Quinta. Quinta had stolen Celia Farnsworth from him, and in his own crazed way Talbot blamed the gunfighter for what was about to happen.

"Take him!" the cattle baron told his *segundo*.

"Guess it's just you and me, Dixon," said Zachery.

"Hold it, Zachery!"

The voice of the gunfighter Moses Quinta froze Zachery's gun hand, and he edged his horse sideways, as did the cattle baron, who paled when he realized that

Quinta was no more than fifty yards away. He studied Quinta, and Talbot felt a stab of resentment when he saw that the man he'd once called a friend had aged well. There Celia Farnsworth was too, a few yards behind Quinta, the woman who'd spurned his love. Now! his mind screamed, now was the time to get it over with.

"You were a damned fool, Quinta, to side with that woman," he said bitterly.

"Guess I've got to learn things the hard way."

As Talbot's hand inched toward his gun, he shouted, "We've got them outnumbered, men!"

"Keep your weapons leathered!" came Bill Liscomb's shout, and when the hired guns glanced over their shoulders, it was to find that they were covered by Liscomb and his men.

"You'll pay for this, Liscomb," Talbot said. "You're fired—so damn it, clear out of here!"

"It'll back your play," Pat Zachery said recklessly. His quick grin spanned the distance between himself and a waiting Moses Quinta. "They say you've got quite a reputation, Quinta. Or is this more brag than fact?"

"Only one way to find out, runt."

"Draw, you sonofa—" Zachery palmed his Colt .45 and was clearing leather with it when a slug from Quinta's gun bored into his right shoulder. The hard impact threw his aim off, the bullet he meant for Quinta tugging at the man's hat. Cursing away the pain, Zachery steadied his gun to fire it again, only to stiffen in the saddle as another slug tore out his right eye, and the spark of life went out of the other one.

Moses Quinta heard a rifle bark at his side before he glanced that way to find that Celia was holding it. She was levering another shell into the breech of her rifle when her bronc neighed in agony and stumbled to its knees, throwing Celia to the ground.

"Now it's your turn to die, Quinta!" screamed out the cattle baron as he spurred his horse forward.

His eyes lidding angrily, Quinta placed the remaining bullets in his revolver into Charlton Talbot's midsection. As the cattle baron dropped out of the saddle, his boot hooked into a stirrup, and his horse bolted southward, dragging the man's lifeless body.

Reining toward the hired guns, Moses Quinta said flatly, "I'm giving you until sundown to clear out of the territory." And grimly he watched as those who'd done Charlton Talbot's killing rode away in scattered bunches or alone. They wouldn't be back, he knew, these scum who sold their loyalty and guns to the highest bidder. It was the stayers, such as Hank Willard, Jud Walker and yes, Raoul Dixon, who would finally determine the destiny of this place called Wyoming territory.

The feeling came to Moses Quinta, too, that his gunfighting days were over, as was his stay up here. It had been a nice dream while it lasted, him and Celia getting together. But she had troubles enough, what with rebuilding the 77 spread and worrying about three marriageable daughters than to saddle herself with an unregenerate gunfighter. So once he settled his accounts with Mrs. Farnsworth when they got to Sheridan, Quinta's notion was to head for that Grand Teton country, with his dream now of opening that gambling house.

"Yup, poker's a fever hard to shake."

21

There was no music sweeter to Moses Quinta's ears than a deck of cards being riffled, or the pungent aroma of cigar smoke and a bottle of brandy at his elbow, with no woman like Mrs. Farnsworth to tell him no. This high-stakes game going on in one of the Elephant Bar's back rooms had interrupted his journey toward that Grand Teton country. But at the moment Quinta wasn't complaining, having just taken in three pots running.

Lamplight was plentiful in the boxlike room decorated with faded wallpaper spangled with garlands of roses and a metal corrugated ceiling showing signs of leakage, but what really brightened up its interior was Sheila, one of the bar girls, rouged and otherwise painted up to make her look about twenty but who was actually heading for her early forties. She'd been keeping them supplied with smokes and liquor, and had been wanting to take Quinta up to her room ever since he'd ridden in four days ago.

"I'll call that last raise," said a tight-lipped Banker DeWitt. A tall, somewhat thin man with downturned lips under a thick black mustache, Buffalo's only banker had been losing heavily, and most generally when he lost a hand he'd tear up the cards he was holding and demand a new deck. And from the sudden gleam Quinta spotted in the banker's deep-set eyes the man had just been dealt some good cards.

Quinta sipped at the brandy as he studied the cards he held.

"Well, Mr. Quinta," groused the banker, "maybe your luck's running cold."

"Only one way to find out." After Quinta equaled the banker's raise of fifty dollars, he settled his elbows on the arms of his chair and leaned back to study the other players.

The cattle buyer had been breaking about even, as had a local merchant, with both men anteing into the pot. The rancher discarded his hand and picked up his chips, leaving the remaining player, a fancied-up dude clad in black, who claimed to be a gambler out of New Orleans, studying the cards that had been dealt him. The only thing ringing true about the man, mused Quinta, was the thick black beard, for the man was no gambler, and more'n likely someone on the dodge. He had told the other players his name was Dirk Mason, and it rang southern but false, too.

"You in or out?" Banker DeWitt said cuttingly.

"I'll see your fifty," Mason finally said, "and raise you another . . . two hundred."

Quinta hesitated only briefly before matching that last raise. He'd been dealt a pair of sevens, the nine, ten and jack of hearts, which was a good hand to fold on. But Banker DeWitt's complaining manner, and the way this so-called gambler from New Orleans kept giving him the eagle-eye whenever he dealt the cards, had been getting to Quinta. In a friendly game he would have kept the sevens and discarded the other cards, because trying to fill an inside straight was in his opinion as chancy as him ever seeing that Farnsworth woman again. With a guarded smile for those still holding cards, the banker and the gambler from New Orleans, he discarded one of the sevens, and was immediately dealt another card by the banker, who, in turn, kept the cards he'd been dealt, and right away Quinta knew he was bucking a pat hand.

Sliding the card in with the others, Quinta shuffled them in his hands without looking at them, his eyes going under the brim of his hat to the gambler, and when Quinta caught the slight grimace of disgust, he reached for his drink.

Banker DeWitt said, "Well, gentlemen, I believe this is a no-limit game. So I'm betting another thousand dollars."

The gambler, Mason, gritted his teeth and glanced sourly at the banker. "Haven't seen a banker yet that wasn't bluffing." He toyed with his dwindling stack of chips while eying the cards he held.

"I figure you've got a busted hand," said Quinta.

"Luck you've been having," came back the gambler, "just ain't natural."

"Mister," Quinta said coldly, "I don't have to cheat to beat a redneck like you. And while you've been sitting there working up your hate, you didn't notice me arranging my right hand around the butt of my Peacemaker. So I reckon you've got three choices— raise, toss in your hand or go for your weapon."

Slamming his cards down, the man scooped up his chips while glaring across the table at Quinta, who sat there smiling. "You ain't seen the last of me!" He shoved the chair away and left the room.

"So much for southern hospitality," said Quinta to

the banker. "You seem to have dealt yourself a mighty find hand." Slowly his eyes lowered to the cards he was unfolding in his hands, and there was an inward flare of surprise when he discovered that he'd been dealt the eight of hearts, that against all odds and for the first time in his poker-playing days he was holding an inside straight. He'd come close once or twice, lost a lot of money going for one. He blinked a couple of times, refilled his shot glass and drained it while savoring the moment.

"Hmmm," he said around a scowl. "I hate bucking a pat hand. Your raise was a thousand. I'll call that. And maybe the gambler was right about you bluffing me."

"You'll never find out unless you raise the ante."

"Have every intention to. Say—five thousand."

"A delightful bet, sir," chortled the banker. "You don't know how good that makes me feel, Mr. Quinta. It'll be a pleasure getting my money back—and a lot of yours to boot. There is a final raise; shall we say . . . ten thousand?"

"Guess I've never learned to leave well enough alone," murmured Quinta, and hesitating as he looked at his pile of chips. "They say you should never buck a man on his home turf."

"So I've heard," Banker DeWitt said confidently.

"Well, another ten does it."

Laughing, the banker spread out his cards on the green table top. "Sorry, sir, but I've four natural kings." His eyes and hands slid greedily toward the chips spread out on the table.

"Afraid that ain't good enough," said Quinta, revealing his cards.

The banker seemed to have shriveled lower on his

chair. "I—I can't believe it. . . ." His left hand began trembling as he reached toward Quinta's cards to determine if he'd read them right, and then he jerked his hand back to turn accusing eyes upon the man who'd just bested him.

"Poker is like that," Quinta said somberly.

"Maybe—maybe that gambler . . . was right," mumbled Banker DeWitt.

"The only one Quinta cheated was me!"

The occupants of the room looked toward the open doorway where Celia Farnsworth stood pointing a cocked Smith & Wesson at them. She stepped further into the room. "Everyone but Quinta clear out of here!"

"But—but—"

"You'd best leave, Banker DeWitt," warned Quinta. "It's me this lady's after. Believe me, Celia Farnsworth ain't too particular about who she fills with lead."

The banker and the other players picked up what chips they had left and scurried past Celia and out into the hallway. Slamming the door shut, she turned angry eyes upon Quinta again.

Removing his hat, Quinta tossed it upon an empty chair and spat out, "Now, Mrs. Farnsworth, what's this about me cheating you?"

"You did, Mr. Quinta." Celia came over to the table. "The only way I'm going to get back what you took is to engage you in a game of poker. Winner take all!"

"That's just fine and dandy." He spread out his arms while glaring up at her. "But just what in—"

"Watch your language, Mr. Quinta."

"Just what in tarnation did I steal from you?"

"My love, Mr. Quinta."

His eyes gaped wider. "I don't reckon I done heard

221

right, Mrs. Farnsworth."

"Don't get sassy with me, Quinta. You heard right, alright. Now here's the way of it. If I win all of your money you've got to marry me."

"You've got some gall! You best me in poker? Why—"

"I don't intend to lose, Mr. Quinta."

"Of all the blue blazes nerve! Woman, if you don't beat all."

"High card deals, Moses." Celia Farnsworth sat down across from the man she had come to love.

"So be it, Celia."

THE UNTAMED WEST
brought to you by Zebra Books

THE LAST MOUNTAIN MAN   (1480, $2.25)
by William W. Johnstone

He rode out West looking for the men who murdered his father and brother. When an old mountain man taught him how to kill a man a hundred different ways from Sunday, he knew he'd make sure they all remembered . . . THE LAST MOUNTAIN MAN.

SAN LOMAH SHOOTOUT   (1853, $2.50)
by Doyle Trent

Jim Kinslow didn't even own a gun, but a group of hardcases tried to turn him into buzzard meat. There was only one way to find out why anybody would want to stretch his hide out to dry, and that was to strap on a borrowed six-gun and ride to death or glory.

TOMBSTONE LODE   (1915, $2.95)
by Doyle Trent

When the Josey mine caved in on Buckshot Dobbs, he left behind a rich vein of Colorado gold—but no will. James Alexander, hired to investigate Buckshot's self-proclaimed blood relations learns too soon that he has one more chance to solve the mystery and save his skin or become another victim of TOMBSTONE LODE.

GALLOWS RIDERS   (1934, $2.50)
by Mark K. Roberts

When Stark and his killer-dogs reached Colby, all it took was a little muscle and some well-placed slugs to run roughshod over the small town—until the avenging stranger stepped out of the shadows for one last bloody showdown.

DEVIL WIRE   (1937, $2.50)
by Cameron Judd

They came by night, striking terror into the hearts of the settlers. The message was clear: Get rid of the devil wire or the land would turn red with fencestringer blood. It was the beginning of a brutal range war.

Available wherever paperbacks are sold, or order direct from the Publisher. Send cover price plus 50¢ per copy for mailing and handling to Zebra Books, Dept. 1975, 475 Park Avenue South, New York, N.Y. 10016. Residents of New York, New Jersey and Pennsylvania must include sales tax. DO NOT SEND CASH.

GREAT WESTERNS
by Dan Parkinson

GUNPOWDER GLORY   (1448, $2.50)

Jeremy Burke, breaking a deathbed promise to his pa, killed the lowdown Sutton boy who was the cause of his pa's death. But when the bullets started flying, he found there was more at stake than his own life as innocent people were caught in the crossfire of *Gunpowder Glory*.

BLOOD ARROW   (1549, $2.50)

Randall Kerry returned to his camp to find his companion slaughtered and scalped. With a war cry as wild as the savages', the young scout raced forward with his pistol held high to meet them in battle.

BROTHER WOLF   (1728, $2.95)

Only two men could help Lattimer run down the sheriff's killers — a stranger named Stillwell and an Apache who was as deadly with a Colt as he was with a knife. One of them would see justice done — from the muzzle of a six-gun.

CALAMITY TRAIL   (1663, $2.95)

Charles Henry Clayton fled to the west to make his fortune, get married and settle down to a peaceful life. But the situation demanded that he strap on a six-gun and ride toward a showdown of gunpowder and blood that would send him galloping off to either death or glory on the . . . *Calamity Trail*.

SUNDOWN BREED   (1860, $2.95)

The last thing Darby Curtis wanted was an Indian war. But a ruthless bunch of land-grabbers wanted the high plains to themselves, even if it meant flaming an Indian uprising. Darby found himself in a deadly crossfire of hot lead. The Kiowa were out for blood . . . and the blood they wanted was his.

Available wherever paperbacks are sold, or order direct from the Publisher. Send cover price plus 50¢ per copy for mailing and handling to Zebra Books, Dept. 1975, 475 Park Avenue South, New York, N.Y. 10016. Residents of New York, New Jersey and Pennsylvania must include sales tax. DO NOT SEND CASH.